RISE
OF THE
OUTLAW QUEEN

THE LIGHTNING SPHERE REPORTS

RISE
OF THE
OUTLAW QUEEN

ERIN C. J. HANEY

God,

You convinced me I could run when I had only ever walked,

you stayed beside me when I fell behind the pack,

and you were the one in the distance

motivating me to cross the finish line.

Every step has been because of you.

Thank you!

CONTENTS

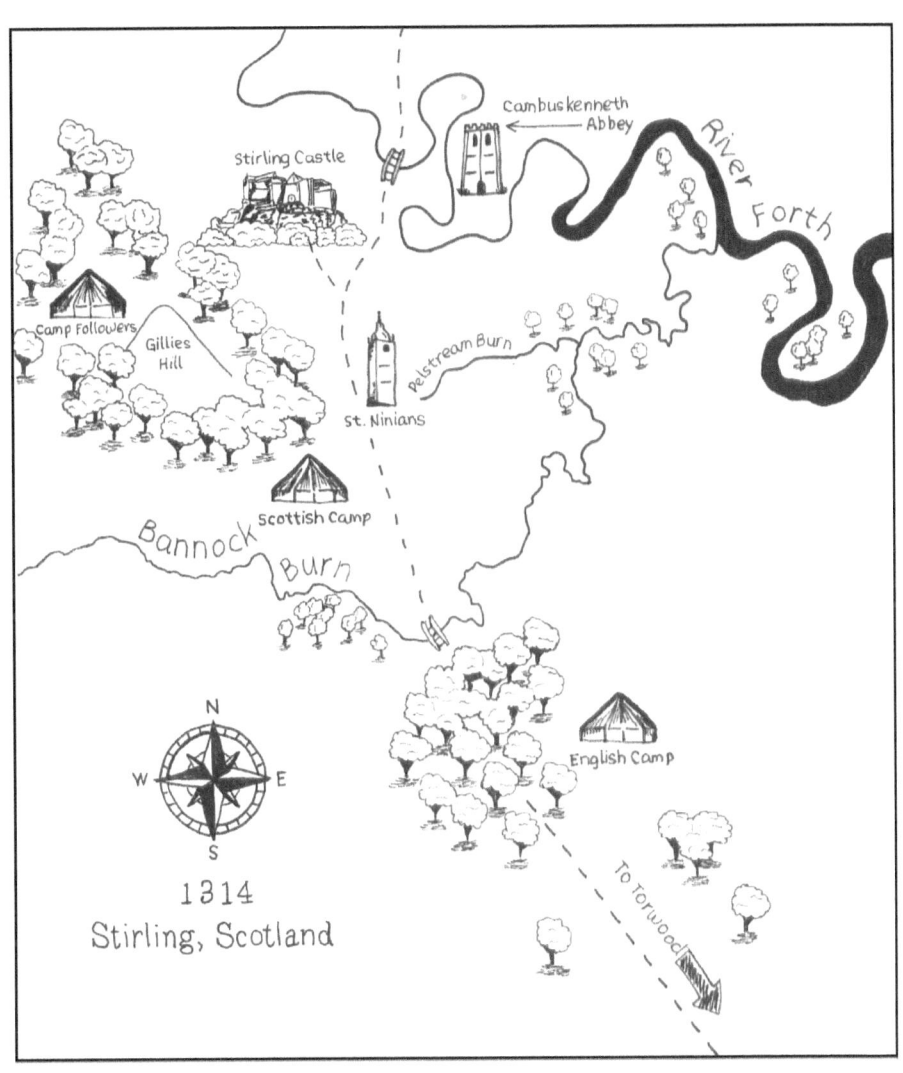

x

1

AVA

"Who's that?" I heard a girl whisper.

"That's the new girl," her friend replied in tone that made it clear it wasn't a compliment. I pretended I heard nothing as I walked past them and up a flight of stone steps toward a building so old, and so massive, that I could almost pretend it was on a college campus. Almost.

As I reached the top of the stairs, the building's doors burst open and a group of young girls rushed out. They were laughing and smiling. Then they saw me. Their laughter stopped and their faces froze before they huddled tightly together and ran down the remaining steps.

With the large wooden doors now before me, I suddenly couldn't move. I knew I had to open those doors, but I didn't want to. I stared at the handles. They were an antique gold color and at the top of each one, was a lion's head. The lions bared their teeth in mid-roar and looked at me with ferocious eyes that seemed to glow when the sunlight hit them. The rest of the door handle curved like a question mark except at the end, instead of a dot, there was a lion's paw.

I felt like the biblical Daniel about ready to walk into the lion's den. But unlike the lions in Daniel's story, I was pretty sure the beasts inside were about to eat me alive.

Don't let them see you sweat. Taking a deep breath I squared my shoulders, lifted my chin, and flung open the doors.

Once inside, I was greeted with a blast of cold air. The heavy mahogany doors slammed behind me as my eyes adjusted to the dim lighting. Instantly, I wished they hadn't. What I saw was terrifying. Words cannot even describe the horror. Before me was a sea of students—both boys and girls—wearing the ugliest uniforms I had ever had the misfortune of laying my eyes on.

I knew they were going to be bad. The few students I had passed coming in had been wearing the revolting things. However, nothing could have prepared me for the sight of seemingly hundreds of students wearing the hideous creations all at once. The girls were wearing knee-length skirts in green plaid, white button-up blouses, a green plaid tie, navy knee-high socks, and a navy blazer with trimming in the same hideous plaid. The blazer had a patch of the school coat-of-arms sewn onto the left side. The boys were dressed almost identical except instead of skirts and knee-high socks, they wore either navy or khaki pants. I was surprised they were wearing pants though; with all that plaid I half expected them to be wearing Scottish kilts!

Normally, I would have found the outfits funny. Unfortunately, it occurred to me that I would soon be forced to wear one. *Why did my dad have to send me to a boarding school that required uniforms? Wasn't sending me to boarding school punishment enough?* Evidently not.

As I made my way toward the headmaster's office at the end of the hall, the judgmental stares and muffled gossiping continued. I wasn't used to all the attention I was getting. In fact, I had spent most of my life feeling practically invisible.

Of my parent's three children, I am the middle child. My older sister, Rebecca, is a straight-A student who is the definition of responsibility. My younger sister, Emma, is cute . . . too cute. Angora bunnies wish they could be as cute. Compared to my sisters, my C-average grades and average looks just could not compete. At least according to my dad and almost everyone else in my life. My mom was the one exception. She noticed me.

I used to desperately wish that other people noticed me too. Now, though, looking around at the sea of snooty plaid, and piercing eyes, I was starting to regret that wish.

After escaping into the headmaster's office, I was greeted with a friendly, "Hello, Ava," from an attractive blonde woman with a beautiful white smile. "I'm Julie, welcome to Providence Academy," she said, smiling. "Would you like a cookie?" Still smiling, she offered me a tray of cookies labeled "organic and gluten-free." *Fancy!*

"Uh . . . no thanks. I'm good. Are you the headmaster?"

"Oh, goodness no," she chuckled. "I'm the receptionist." I noticed she was still smiling, which led me to believe that she either really liked her job or else she really liked her teeth. "Follow me, I'll show you to her office."

She led me behind her desk and down a back hallway. When we reached the headmaster's office, she knocked a couple times before opening the door. "Dr. Hendrickson, Ava's here to see you," she announced.

"Come in," the headmaster replied, sitting with perfect posture in her leather chair. She clasped her hands together and rested them on her elaborate wooden desk. Although she was an older woman (probably in her 70's), she had strength in her eyes as she evaluated me from behind her glasses.

Julie left and I had a sudden urge to run after her. "Close the door and have a seat, Ava." With some hesitancy, I followed her instructions.

"I'm Agatha Hendrickson, though you may call me Dr. Hendrickson."

"You're not a shrink or anything, are you?" I asked.

"I'm not *that* kind of doctor," she corrected, clearly not amused. There was something in her tone that made me feel like I should probably keep my mouth shut. I was glad, though, that I had asked. My father had taken me to several psychiatrists over the last year and I had no desire to talk to another one.

"I've spoken with your father," she continued, "and the judge."

Oh boy, here we go!

"Yes, I have heard all about your recent . . . activities."

That's a nice way of putting it.

"They both seem to think it would be in your best interest for you to receive more academic and social structure in your life. Here at Providence Academy, we pride ourselves on giving our young boys and girls just that."

Can't wait. I squirmed in my chair, trying to get comfortable, knowing that the lecture was far from over and that I was going to have to be present for every painful minute of it.

"Our students here are exceptional," she said.

By "exceptional" she meant that the students were either exceptionally smart or their parents had an exceptional amount of money. For most of them, it was because of the money. I couldn't judge, though. My family has a lot of money and it wasn't much of a secret that the only reason I was accepted into the academy was because of the large financial "donation" my dad made to the school. The next few sentences out of the headmaster's mouth only confirmed that fact.

"We strive to keep our students performing at an exceptional level. Now, I would be lying if I said that I was completely confident that you belong here. If it were not for your father's *persuasiveness*, I would have recommended a different placement."

I was sure that was true. If it was up to her, my placement would have probably included bars and an orange onesie.

"However, you are with us now. Therefore, there are a few ground rules that need to be established. First, I expect you to be on your best behavior while you are here at Providence. Anything less will not be tolerated. If you have any questions on what type of behavior we expect, I refer you to the student handbook." She opened her desk drawer, pulled out a large green book with the school coat of arms on the cover, and dropped it on the desk in front of me. It landed with a *thunk*.

"In addition," she continued, "although this is a co-ed school, we do not have co-ed dorms. Boys are not allowed into the girls' dormitory and vice versa. If you are caught breaking this rule you will be expelled. Do I make myself clear?"

I nodded.

"Good. During the school week, uniforms are required. Yours are waiting for you in your dorm room. On the weekends, you are free to wear what you desire . . . within limits." Keeping her chin up, she lowered her eyes to look down at my ripped jeans and muddy high-tops with a disapproving gaze. I doubted my outfit was against the rules. It was just against her idea of lady-like attire. "If you have any questions on the subject, I will again refer you to the student handbook. Do you have any questions?"

I shook my head.

Dr. Hendrickson pressed an intercom button, "Julie, bring Miss McAdam in please."

A few moments later, a tiny girl with curly red hair bounced into the office. She had tried to tie up the unruly locks into a ballerina bun, but

4

several strands had broken free and were left dancing around her face. She didn't bother moving them out of the way.

"Ava, this is Cassidy," Dr. Hendrickson announced. "She has been with us for four years now and is a member of our welcoming committee. She is also president of the Public Speaking Club and is one of our top students in science and math. Like you, she is a part of this year's freshman class, so she will be able to show you around and help you get used to the Providence way of life." After a brief pause, she added briskly, "You two may see yourselves out."

What a relief it was stepping out of that woman's office! The instant I left the building, it was as if the air smelled sweeter and the sun shone brighter. Sweet release!

However, as Cassidy and I made our way around campus, it became painfully obvious why she was the president of the Public Speaking Club. She wouldn't stop talking!

"Over there is the cafeteria." She quickly added, "I don't know what you like to eat, but whatever you like I'm sure they have it. They have different eating stations to choose from and they feature food from around the world. They've served American food, Italian food, Chinese food, Mexican food, Greek food, Turkish food. My favorite is the Korean food. It took me awhile to get used to the spiciness, but now I could eat Korean dukbokki every day!"

She continued voicing her love for food, at incredible speed, for another 10 minutes straight. To be clear, I didn't have anything against her. She seemed pretty nice. In fact, she was the first student I had seen all day that didn't take one look at me and frown. I just wished she'd take a breath!

"If you'll follow me this way," she directed, "I'll show you where the girls' dormitory is. Can you believe we're on the same floor?"

I opened my mouth to reply, but evidently it was a rhetorical question because she didn't wait for an answer.

"You're gonna love it! It's located really close to the church, so unlike the boys who are located all the way on the other side of campus, we can get in an extra few minutes of sleep on Sunday mornings. Unless, of course, you're one of those people who spends a lot of time on their hair. Not me! I'd much rather sleep!"

I knew Providence was a private Christian boarding school, but for some reason it hadn't occurred to me that I would have to attend church. Although I considered myself a Christian, it had been a long time since I'd so much as stepped foot inside a church, and I wasn't sure I wanted to start now.

I allowed my mind to wander back to what those Sundays used to be like. Because it was our cook's day off, my mom would get up early and make us a huge stack of her special Sunday pancakes with chocolate sauce, powdered sugar, and strawberries on top. Then, my sisters and I would go to Sunday school before joining our parents for the service. I remembered how I used to race my sisters as hard as I could so I was sure to sit next to my mom. Then I'd snuggle up next to her on the pew and she'd put her arm around me. I missed that. After she passed away, my dad stopped taking us to church. Truth be told, he stopped doing much of anything with us.

Suddenly, my eyes started stinging. I knew I had to put a stop to thoughts of the past, or risk embarrassing myself by crying. I could not let that happen.

Cutting Cassidy off mid-sentence I exclaimed, "What's that building over there?" I had no idea what she had been talking about and I really didn't care. In order to switch topics, I just picked a random building and pointed to it. As it so happened, the building looked abandoned and had large metal chains locked around the door handles.

"That's the old science building." Her energetic attitude evaporated and I detected a note of fear in her voice. "You don't want to go in there."

"Why? Is it haunted?" I said laughing.

"Yes," she said very seriously.

I waited a moment to see if she started laughing too, but she didn't. "That's ridiculous," I corrected. "There's no such thing as ghosts or haunted buildings. Those are just stories people tell kids to try to scare them."

"Oh really?"

"Really."

"Then how do you explain Dr. Keller?"

I sighed, "I don't know. Who's Dr. Keller?"

"Dr. Keller was a teacher here in the 1970's. He was the head of the science department and his office was in that very building."

"So what? Did he hear strange noises? Did his beakers get moved around?"

"Very funny," she said sarcastically. "Dr. Keller wasn't *haunted* by ghosts. He *is* the ghost. Legend has it that he was obsessed with science. Every day after work, he would lock himself up in his lab and do secret experiments. Nobody knew what they were, but some say that when there were thunderstorms, they would hear a loud *whoosh* sound and the faint screech of a train . . . or a scream."

She was telling the story so dramatically, that I had to bite the inside of my lip to control my urge to laugh. If Cassidy wasn't already in the Drama Club, she really should be. I let her continue the story, but hoped she would end it before my lip started to bleed.

"Then one day, during the biggest storm of the year, Dr. Keller went into his lab and never . . . came . . . out! They looked for him, but after a while, they gave up and declared him dead. In his will, he left his fortune to the school's science department. So, they built a new science building and abandoned the old one. Some say, though, that the reason they used the money to build a new building was because he had never really left the old one. . . ."

"Well, as fascinating as that story is, isn't it possible that there is a reasonable explanation for it all?"

"Like what?!" she screamed indignantly. "How do you explain his disappearance?"

"Maybe he just left. Maybe he had some personal problems in his life and, instead of confronting them, he decided to run away."

"But they declared him dead!"

"So? Maybe they made a mistake. Maybe he wanted it that way. For all we know, he was running from the mob and is now living out in the woods somewhere playing Davy Crockett."

"Okay . . . well . . ." she hesitated, "why did they build a new science building?"

"Because they finally had the money for it and the old one was *old*. I mean, look at it!" Indeed, the building had seen better days. Several of the windows had been smashed out and its stone steps were cracked and tilting into the earth. Ivy had overtaken a large portion of its brick walls, like thin

7

fingers trying to pull the heavy building into the ground. Looking at it now, it wasn't hard to see why some people might think it was haunted.

"It didn't look like that when they locked it up," Cassidy said. "Anyway, I do get your point. But there's one thing that you can't explain!"

"What's that?"

"The strange noises."

"You mean the *whoosh* and the train sound?"

"Yep!"

"Well, wind often *whooshes* during a storm."

"True . . ."

"And, call me crazy, but I'm thinking a train sound could be from— follow me now—a train!"

"We don't have any trains here."

"What do you mean?"

"I mean, we don't have any trains here. The nearest train is like, thirty miles from here. We don't hear it on the quietest of nights, let alone during a noisy thunderstorm."

I was both shocked and stumped. Surely there had to be an explanation, but I couldn't think of one off the top of my head. "Uh . . . well . . . I don't know, but . . ."

"Hah!" she exclaimed. "You see, it's haunted!"

"I don't . . ."

"I know you don't want to admit when you're wrong, and I'm sure you don't want to go to a school with a ghost. Neither do I, but as long as we avoid that building, we should be fine."

That wasn't even close to how I was going to finish that sentence, but I decided to let it go. Feeling like she had won the debate, she switched topics and continued leading me on her tour of the campus. As I started to follow her, I took a moment to take one last look at the crumbling old building. Despite the fact that I found there to be a mysterious beauty to the wreckage, I did wonder why they never tore it down.

2

AVA

"Home sweet home," Cassidy said dramatically as she threw open the door of my dorm room and ushered me inside. So far, although I didn't want to admit it, I had actually been pretty impressed with the girls' dormitory. The student lounges and hallways were decorated in the modern colonial style. Dark wood, gold finishes, and wingback chairs gave warmth to the trendy grey walls. What I really liked were the occasional pops of red (my favorite color) around the rooms.

As I stepped into my room, I was pleasantly surprised. It wasn't quite as nice as the common areas, but it was still nice. The walls were grey, but the ceiling was white. Normally, I would find that boring. What saved it for me, though, were the windows. On the far end of the room, were four narrow windows that, when put together, created one large window. They were surrounded by an aged wooden frame and adorned with a stained-glass banner across the top. They were the kind of windows I could imagine being in a castle.

I walked over to them and looked out. Being on the top floor of the dormitory provided a great view of the campus. I could see the school entrance gates in the distance, flanked by rows of trees beginning to change color. The path led toward the main building that, truth be told, was more attractive from the front than from the back. I kind of felt like telling it to turn around. Close to the main building, the church's majestic steeple shot into the sky. I also had a fairly clear view of several academic buildings, including the crumbling old science building. Although I didn't believe Cassidy's crazy ghost story, I still found the prospect of living so close to it a little unsettling. Maybe the most unsettling part was that I wasn't sure why I felt that way.

Quickly, I turned around and assessed the rest of the room. An industrial ceiling light with exposed Edison bulbs hung down from the ceiling. On each side of the room was a twin bed, a wall-facing desk, and a closet with sliding doors near the entrance. On the back of the front door, there was a mirror.

Though my side had yet to be decorated, whoever my roommate was had styled hers in shades of pale pink and blue with touches of fluffy white fabric. She had a large picture of Paris on the wall next to her bed. In front of her desk, she had hung a large vanity mirror framed with light bulbs. As for the desk itself, I couldn't help but notice that it was covered in more makeup than study materials. There was something about the ultra-feminine design mixed with the immaculate cleanliness that gave me a sinking feeling in my stomach. *This girl is not going to like me.*

"So, what do you think?" Cassidy asked.

"It's nice," I said nonchalantly. "It's a room."

"Well, it will feel more like home when they deliver your stuff and you're able to put your own 'personal touch' on the room."

"Yeah, I guess."

"Hey," she said full of excitement, "I know what will really make you feel at home!"

"What?"

"Try on your uniform!"

Was she kidding? What part of skipping around, looking like a cheerleader for Scotch tape, was supposed to make me feel at home? "Uh . . . I'm good, thanks," I said hoping she would change topics.

"Oh, come on! *Please,*" she whined. "I just know you'll feel like one of us as soon as you put it on. Besides, you'll have to wear it to go to supper anyway."

I sighed, knowing I wasn't going to escape my fate. "Fine," I mumbled. I went over to the closet and slid it open. There it was, in all its glory, waiting for me. When I was little, my parents used to tell me again and again that there were no such things as monsters in the closet. They lied.

"Uh, Cassidy," I said looking toward her, "can I get some privacy?"

"Oh, yeah! Of course! Duh," she said hitting herself on the head. "If you need me or have any questions, my dorm is right across the hall. Otherwise, I'll see you at supper." As she opened the door to leave, two girls walked by, looked in at me, and started whispering to each other. This was getting ridiculous!

"Actually, Cassidy, I do have a question."

"What's that?"

"I get the feeling that everybody here knows about me, and not in a good way. I have a feeling you know, too." The smile faded from her face and her eyes avoided my gaze. I knew I was on the right track, so I continued. "What I want to know is, how does everybody know? Was it printed in the school newspaper? Was there an alert that rang in on everyone's phones reading 'WARNING: REBELLIOUS TEEN COMES TO TOWN'?"

"No, of course not! Nothing that obvious."

"Then how?"

Cassidy cautiously looked around the hall, came in, and closed the door. "Tessa Mueller."

"Who's Tessa Mueller?"

"She's the daughter of the woman in charge of admissions. Her mother knows everything about everyone."

"And her mom just tells her?"

"I'm assuming, but I don't know for sure. It doesn't really matter, though. As soon as Tessa gets hold of information, you can bet the entire school is going to know about it."

"Great," I said sarcastically. There was nothing I disliked more than people talking about me behind my back. I have always preferred that people tell me to my face if they have a problem with me. Unfortunately, most people are too afraid to do that. It's more comfortable for them to spread gossip when their victims aren't around.

"Also, I should warn you," Cassidy said, "Tessa is best friends with your new roomie, so I'd be careful what you . . ."

At that very moment, the door swung open. Standing in the doorway was a tall girl with long-grey hair. Obviously, grey was not her God-given color, but she pulled it off. In combination with her upturned nose and diamond-studded manicure, she looked almost like a fairy. The only thing that was unattractive about her was her bad attitude.

She narrowed her eyes at me and slowly stepped into the room. "Well, well, well," she began, "the criminal has finally arrived."

"Maci!" Cassidy shouted in horror.

"What?" Maci asked with feigned innocence. "She is, isn't she?"

"That's not the point," Cassidy mumbled, as if I wasn't going to hear her.

"I think it is the point. Especially since she's going to be staying in my room instead of in a jail cell." She turned and looked at me. "In case you're thinking of stealing from me, don't." Reaching her arm out, she flung open her closet door. Immediately, an alarm started blaring. Cassidy and I covered our ears.

"WHAT'S THAT?" Cassidy yelled over the noise.

Maci made a show of raising a clicker in the air and pressing the button. The noise stopped. She smirked.

"That, my friends, is a burglar alarm. Try to steal from me, and I'll know it."

I wanted to say something to her, something that would make her eat her words, something that would prove how wrong she was about me, but my mind came up empty. If I argued, I would have to talk about what I did and why I did it and, truth be told, I really didn't feel like explaining myself to someone so smug and judgmental. I could see she had already formed her opinion about me and there wasn't much I could do to change that.

"I just came for my bag," she said as she pulled out a pink Gucci backpack and slung it over one shoulder. She then closed the closet door and set the alarm. As she made her way out the door, she left us with one final thought, "And do yourself a favor Jailbird—stay out of my way."

Cassidy looked at me with concern. "Hey, don't let Maci get to you. She's not really a people person."

"Sure, no sweat." I tried to muster a smile, but I doubted it was very convincing.

"Well," she said, visibly unsure of what to say, "I'll let you get changed."

As she was leaving, I felt compelled to ask her one more question. "Hey Cassidy!"

"Yeah?"

"Why are you so nice to me?"

She paused a moment before answering, "Why wouldn't I be? I don't even know you yet." She smiled, and then closed the door.

Cassidy wasn't kidding about the food. They had a lot of options that all looked amazing! I was debating between the chicken and waffles or the Vietnamese pho, when I heard a familiar voice shout, "Hey Ava, over here!"

I turned and saw tiny Cassidy bouncing up and down, waiving her arms in the air, trying to get my attention. Slightly embarrassed, I reciprocated with a small wave and a head nod to let her know I was aware of her presence. I liked her, but she was making my plan of keeping a low profile somewhat difficult.

I hurriedly grabbed the chicken and waffles and headed over. She was sitting with a girl who had straight, jet-black hair. That was all I could see of her. The rest of her face was buried in a book.

"Look at you rocking that uniform!" Cassidy squealed. "How do you feel?"

"Like I've lost my dignity."

"Oh, don't be silly, you look darling!"

Was there a worse compliment for a 15-year-old girl than being called "darling?" It made me feel like an overgrown Shirley Temple. Self-consciously, I tugged at the tie around my neck, trying to loosen its grip.

"Have a seat, Ava. I want to introduce you to my roommate, and best friend, Winnie." The girl with the dark hair lowered her book.

"Hi," she said quietly. Though the word was directed toward me, she refused to make eye contact.

"Winnie and I both came to Providence around the same time," Cassidy explained. "She was nervous about having a roommate at first, since she's an only child, but then she realized I'm awesome. Right, Winnie?"

Winnie smiled shyly, but continued to look away. I wanted to grab her face and ask, "Winnie, are you being held against your will? Blink once for 'yes' and twice for 'no.'"

Though the thought amused me, I knew better. Her timid reaction had nothing to do with the fact that she was living with a chatterbox. They seemed to be opposites that would complement each other well. No, I was certain it was meeting me that was the source of her nerves. In an attempt to break the ice, I asked, "So, what are you reading?"

Silently, she raised her book up so that I could get a look at the title.

"The Chronicles of Narnia," I read aloud, *"The Lion, the Witch, and the Wardrobe.* Good choice. I love that book! After I read it, I was obsessed with the idea of being able to step into a wardrobe and enter a magical world. In fact, when I was younger, my sisters and I used to dress up in our winter clothes and pretend to be the characters. My older sister, Rebecca, would be Susan and my little sister, Emma, would be Lucy. It was a lot of fun!"

"What part did you play?" Cassidy asked.

Frowning, I mumbled, "Edmund." Cassidy burst out laughing and Winnie smiled wide enough to show teeth. It was an improvement. "Hey, it isn't my fault only two of the kids in the book are girls! You take what you can get! Anyway, it was still fun. That is, until my mom made us stop playing."

"Why would she do that?" Winnie asked meekly.

"Because we kept leaping from the closets and scaring the housekeepers."

Again, they laughed. It wasn't long before the awkwardness was gone and we were all talking like real friends. I ended up learning a lot about them. For instance: I learned that Cassidy has an older brother who is in the military, that she hates math even though she is really good at it, and that she wanted a puppy so badly that she got caught trying to sneak a stray into her dorm room. I also noticed that she must love traveling since her backpack was covered with enamel pins from all over the world.

Unsurprisingly, Winnie was a tougher nut to crack. She did mention, though, that she reads a lot of books of various genres and that she likes watching old black-and-white films. It wasn't a lot of information to go on, but it did tell me that she has an impressive attention span. I had been forced to sit through a few black-and-white movies over the years, but never once was I successful at staying awake long enough to see the endings.

14

Overall, my first meal at Providence was really pleasant. That is, until dessert. Cassidy selected a slice of strawberry cheesecake. Winnie chose a bowl of chocolate mousse. And I found a beautifully crunchy cannoli that had my name written all over it. But as soon as we had made our selections and sat down with our sugary treats before us, I heard someone scream, "GO LONG!" I turned my head just in time to see a football whizz past my face and land directly into Winnie's bowl of chocolate mousse. The impact flung the fluffy chocolate all over Winnie's white shirt. Next, the chocolate-covered football skidded, knocking over a full glass of milk before coming to a stop in Winnie's lap. The milk cascaded over the edge of the table, landing in puddles around her feet.

The cafeteria erupted in a fit of laughter. Students were pointing and standing on their chairs to get a better view. Some even pulled out their cell phones to take photos of the aftermath.

Winnie, however, was not laughing. Her lip began to tremble and her eyes turned red. Pretty soon, she lost all ability to hold back the tears. Lowering her head, she allowed her hair to cover her tear-streaked face.

With almost mother-like authority, Cassidy grabbed the napkins off the table and led her friend out of the cafeteria, away from the crowd.

Seeing Winnie break down in front of me was bad enough, but what really made me mad was turning around to see who had thrown the ball. Standing in the far-left aisle of the cafeteria were two boys. The tallest boy had blonde hair, blue eyes, and an athletic build. The other was only slightly shorter, with dark brown hair and a mischievous smile. Under normal circumstances, I would have said that both boys were mildly attractive. However, these were not normal circumstances, and all I could see when I looked over at them were two boys doubled over, laughing.

I couldn't believe it. Those boys had made that poor girl cry. Were they apologetic? Were they embarrassed? Did they look upset in any way? No! They actually had the audacity to laugh!

After arriving at Providence, I promised myself that I would keep a low profile. I would go to class, stay quiet, and avoid trouble. So far, I had kept that promise for about three hours. That seemed long enough.

3

NOLAN

The pass, the fumble, and then right into the chocolate. . . .
TOUCHDOWN! Every time I thought I was done laughing, my mind
replayed the scene, and it started all over again. Doubled over from
laughing so hard, I managed to spit out, "Can't . . . breathe . . . so funny!"

"Uh-oh," Victor said as he hit me in the side, "angry chick, 12 o'clock."

Sure enough, a brunette with a bad attitude was making her way toward
us. Wiping away the tears that were running down my cheeks, I managed
to pull myself together.

"Which one of you did it?" she seethed through gritted teeth.

Quickly, Victor said, "Don't look at me," with a not-so-subtle point in
my direction. *Tattletale!*

"Thanks man, remind me to return the favor," I said, playfully punching
him in the shoulder.

"So, Blondie," she said looking at me, "what do you have to say for
yourself?"

"Well, first of all, the name's not 'Blondie;' it's Nolan." With a flash of
my signature smile and a wink, I expected her to at least smile back.
Nothing. If anything, she looked even angrier. "As for what I have to say

for myself . . . solid pass, but could use a little more spin next time." I lifted my arms in the air and mimed tossing the ball with perfect form.

"How old are you?" she asked.

"15."

"Then act it!" She uncrossed her arms and angrily pointed at me. "This is a cafeteria, and you're treating it like it's your own personal football field! People come here to eat, not to have footballs thrown at their face!"

"In my defense, I didn't throw it at her face. I threw it at Butterfingers over there," I pointed over at my friend, David, who had retrieved the ball and was now cowering a few feet behind her. She turned to look at him. Once spotted, David nervously fiddled with his glasses and cautiously approached her.

"I'm *so* sorry," David groveled. "I thought I had it, I almost had it, and then . . . I didn't have it. And I'm really sorry about your friend."

The girl's face softened. "That's alright, it was an accident," she said kindly. I guess groveling worked, but there was no way you'd ever catch me doing it!

Attempting to take advantage of her improved mood, I jumped in with, "See, it was all an accident. No harm, no fowl!"

If there had been any thawing of her heart, it had re-frozen as the Ice Queen whipped her head towards me. "*No fowl?*" she enunciated. "You made an innocent girl cry!"

"Look, for that, I'm sorry. Really, I am." I sincerely meant those words, and the honesty had its desired effect. Her face was defrosting. I couldn't help myself, though. With a laugh I added, "But it *was* pretty funny!"

Her eyes flashed with anger and, after grumbling a few unintelligible syllables, she stormed out of the cafeteria.

"HEY! I DIDN'T GET YOUR NAME," I yelled out to her. No response. Turning toward my friends, I chuckled, "She's fun."

Victor scoffed, "Dude, you must have a death wish or somethin'."

"What do you mean?"

"Don't you know who that is?"

"No."

"*She's* the girl Tessa was telling you about in lab."

"I'm afraid you're going to have to be a little bit more specific. I may be Tessa's lab partner, but with her, every night's an episode of Providence TMZ."

"Okay, well how many students has she told you about whose school yearbook photo could be a mug shot?"

"Oh . . ." I said as realization smacked me over the head. "*That's* her?"

"The one and only."

Laughing, I said, "Well that explains the 'angry' eyes."

"Yeah, and you'd better keep them off you, if you know what's good for ya."

"Oh please, like I'd really be scared of her! She might have a bad attitude but I mean, come on, look at her! Like, what'd she even do? Take a candy bar from the local convenience store?"

"Fat chance! From what I heard, she lifted cars and sold them for parts to the local chop shops."

"That's not what I heard," David interjected. "I heard she robbed a bank with her boyfriend, stole a car, and tried to escape to Mexico."

As my friends bickered back and forth (each convinced that they alone knew the true version of the story) I couldn't help but stare in utter shock at the lunacy I was hearing. Finally finding my words, I interrupted, "Listen to yourselves!" David and Victor stopped talking and looked at me. "Victor, it's evident from her being here at Providence that her family has money. Why on earth would she spend her free time selling car parts to chop shops?" Victor was stumped.

"And David," I continued, "what story have you been listening to? Bonnie and Clyde? Butch Cassidy and the Sundance Kid? Get real! Now, I don't know what she did or didn't do, but if there's one thing I've learned from listening to Tessa's incessant drama, it's that Tessa and people like her just love to exaggerate the truth. So, before we jump to conclusions, maybe we should ask her what she did."

"You think she'd tell you?" Victor asked with a smirk. "From what I just saw, I don't think she'll be joining your fan club anytime soon."

"Oh, ye of little faith, it's only a matter of time before she comes to appreciate my unique charm."

"We'll see about that. And speaking of girls who don't appreciate your 'unique charm,'" Victor grabbed my shoulders and spun me around, "your dream girl's over there."

Sitting at one of the tables, surrounded by her group of friends, was the most beautiful girl at Providence. Everything about her was beautiful. Her voice was beautiful, her smile was beautiful, even her name was beautiful . . .

Maci. I just knew that if I could get her to go out with me, I'd be the envy of every guy at school. The only problem was that she was one of the few girls at Providence who didn't want to go out with me.

In all fairness, I'd never officially asked. I'd been waiting for months for the right moment, but it never came. As Maci got up to throw her tray away, Victor slapped me on the back and said, "Now's your chance, Man, show her that signature smile of yours!"

Oh, how I regretted telling him about my signature smile! I should have known he'd use it to tease me. It's what I'd do.

Adjusting my suit jacket, I strode over to where Maci was standing. "Hey Maci, what's up?" My tone was confident and casual. *Good start!*

Maci spun around and flipped her hair. She reciprocated with a smile that rivaled my own. "Oh, hey Nolan! Not much, you?"

"The usual. Hey, so I just discovered that your new roomie is in town."

Instantly, her smile collapsed. "Don't remind me."

"Really?" I asked with feigned surprise. "Because I just met her and she seemed fine—a little *hostile*—but fine."

"Don't be cruel," she replied dryly. "That little hooligan is a blight on the school's reputation and a pain in my butt!"

"She hasn't even been here a day. How big of a pain could she be?"

"Huge! With much effort, I managed to begin this school year having my own room. Now, thanks to a jailbird with deep pockets, I have to SHARE!" Her indignance was palpable.

"Why don't you just get the faculty to move her to another room? Don't tell me you don't have the connections."

She smirked, "You're cute." I felt my heart skip a beat, but reminded myself to stay cool. My relaxed attitude seemed to be working. "Of course I have the connections," she continued. "Unfortunately, they have nowhere else to put her. The dorms are full. I suggested finding her more suitable accommodations, but apparently the horses need the stables."

"Wow," I said laughing, "remind me not to get on your bad side!"

She looked flattered.

This is my chance. We've talked, she's smiled, now all I have to do is ask her to have a cup of coffee with me. No, wait, coffee is too stereotypical. And what if she doesn't like coffee? New plan: I'll ask her if she wants to go for a jog. No, that's a horrible idea! What if she takes it the wrong way and thinks I'm saying she needs to exercise?

That won't work. Dinner! I'll ask her out to dinner. Wait, what am I thinking?! I can't drive and I certainly can't ask her to have dinner with me in the cafeteria.

Suddenly, I was struck with a stroke of genius. *I'll ask her on a picnic! We can eat good food, enjoy nature . . . it's perfect!*

I'd started to open my mouth to ask the question when, all of a sudden, she waved at a person behind me. "Hi Kenny," she squealed. To me she said, "I love his new haircut! He looks so cute!" With that, she flitted off to admire Kenny's hair.

As I watched her leave, all I could think was: *I thought I was cute.*

Out of the corner of my eye, I caught sight of Victor and David laughing and elbowing each other's sides. I knew they had witnessed my epic failure and couldn't wait to let me hear all about it. Sighing, I retreated back to my friends. *This is going to be a long night!*

4

AVA

The walk between the cafeteria and the dormitory did a world of good for my pent-up frustration. I'd known better than to let that irritating boy get under my skin. Yet, here I was, paying the price with high blood pressure. I took a deep breath of the cool fall air, and felt my tension release. The rustling of the trees made a soothing sound. I wished I could stay out there forever—away from the noise, away from the stress, away from the judgment.

As I passed the old science building, I felt compelled to stop for a moment. "Where *did* you go, Dr. Keller?" I asked into the wind. As I looked up at the dilapidated old structure, the breeze tossed leaves across the stone steps and berated its roof with tree limbs, but I received no reply. Shoving my hands deeper into my jacket pockets, I continued on toward the dorms.

Once I'd made it inside, I climbed the steps to the top floor and knocked a few times on Cassidy's door. "Who is it?" she inquired.

"The Big Bad Wolf."

A moment later, the door swung open. Cassidy, who was standing in the doorway, laughed. "Well, your hair kind of makes you look like one right now."

I stepped into the room, closed the door, and looked in the mirror that was hanging on the back of it. Sure enough, the wind had soothed my soul, but *wrecked* my hair. I picked out a leaf that had come along for the ride and ran my fingers through the knotted mess a couple of times. *Good enough.*

Turning around, I walked over to Winnie, who was sitting on the edge of her bed. She had decorated her side of the room in a modern boho look with white bed covers, white macramé wall hangings, and a white orchid on her desk. There were a few touches of pale pink and green added, but not enough to make it feel any less sterile.

Cassidy, on the other hand, decorated her room in vibrant yellow. She had a bouquet of artificial sunflowers on her nightstand and travel pictures, depicting the bright blue waters of Fiji and the fiery red cliffs in Utah, on her walls.

When I sat down next to Winnie, I noticed that her eyes were red and puffy from crying. "So, Winnie . . ." I said awkwardly, "guess you should have gone with the cannoli."

She shot me a look that told me I'd just said the wrong thing.

"Too soon?"

Winnie's only response was a groan, as she flopped back onto the bed and covered her face with her hands.

"Welcome to the party," Cassidy said, throwing her hands up. "I've been trying to tell her it's not a big deal."

Winnie uncovered her face. "How can you say that? I was covered in food. Everyone laughed at me. People took pictures!" With that, she grabbed the pillow next to her and buried her face in it.

Deep in thought, I sauntered over to the window. I understood how Winnie felt, and there was no point in telling her not to feel that way. Even if she shouldn't feel embarrassed, I knew that a simple "stop it" wouldn't suddenly make her feelings go away.

Cassidy and Winnie's window had a much different view than mine. Since it faced the back of the building, it looked out onto the dormitory's patio. On a sunny day, the deck chairs and tables would be a great place to sit and look out onto the rolling, green lawn which led to the woods. Suddenly, I had an idea.

"Get your coat," I demanded.

"What?" Cassidy looked confused.

24

"I said, get your coat. We're going out." Quickly, I strode over to Winnie's desk chair, grabbed the coat she had tossed over it, and threw it to her.

"But I'm in my pajamas," she protested.

Sure enough, Winnie had changed out of her mousse-stained uniform and was now wearing flannel ducky pajamas and slippers that looked like a pair of calico kitties. "It doesn't matter," I said, trying to hurry her along, "just put on a pair of shoes that don't have faces and cover up with your coat."

"But what if someone sees me?"

"You've already had a chocolate-covered photo shoot today. I think the ducks are the least of your worries." Winnie pouted, but complied with my demands.

We were soon sprinting across the back lawn toward the woods. Above us, darkness raced to consume the sky. As the sun faded, the air got colder, but I didn't care. I was warmed with the excitement of a spontaneous adventure.

"WHERE ARE WE GOING?" Cassidy screamed, straining to be heard over the whistle of the wind.

"YOU'LL SEE," I yelled back, not wanting to ruin the surprise.

Once we reached the woods, the sound of the wind was replaced by the snapping of twigs beneath our feet and the occasional hoot of an owl. I pulled out my cell phone and used its light to supplement the moonlight that was struggling to break through the trees. The darkness gave the woods an eerie feeling. It was around this time that I first thought: *What on earth am I doing right now?*

As if reading my mind, Cassidy asked, "Is this really a good idea?"

"This is scary. I want to go back," Winnie whined.

"There's nothing to be scared of, I know what I'm doing. Come on, we're not far." Although not entirely convinced of my confident words, I'd already committed to the mission. Once you've talked someone into leaving the warmth of their room to go trekking through the woods at night in their ducky pajamas, it's really hard to just go, "Oops, my bad. Let's go back now. Hope you enjoyed getting smacked in the face with tree branches for no reason!" Luckily for me, I soon heard the sound I was looking for. Water!

It only took us a few more steps before the trees thinned and we were greeted with a small clearing that surrounded a flowing stream. "We're here," I announced with a dramatic gesture toward the water.

"You took us to a stream," Cassidy said slowly. "*Why?*"

I walked over to the bank, picked up a smooth stone, and put it in Winnie's hand. "Throw it," I directed.

Winnie looked down at the rock and then back at me. "I don't get it," she said at a volume barely above a whisper.

"I want you to think of something that's making you mad and then scream it out as you throw the rock into the stream."

Her eyes darted toward Cassidy, seeking her help, before politely responding, "No thank you." She tried handing the stone back to me, but I wouldn't take it.

"Winnie, throw the rock."

"Wait a minute," Cassidy interjected, "let me get this straight. You had us hike into the woods . . . in the cold . . . at night . . . to throw rocks?"

"Yes, yes I did."

"Ava, I don't mean to be rude, but . . . HAVE YOU LOST YOUR MIND?"

"No, Cassidy, I haven't," I said with frustration. "This girl was just publicly 'moussed.' She's admitted to being embarrassed, and I'm guessing that she's got some anger and frustration buried deep down inside that polite little shell of hers." The more I talked, the more worked up I became. I wasn't crazy and I didn't like people looking at me as if I were. "Now, I don't know a lot of things, and I may only be a C-average student, but if you could get a college degree in anger and frustration then I'd have my Ph.D.! So, if I say this is gonna work, it's gonna work! Now Winnie, THROW THE STUPID ROCK!"

Panicked by my sudden command, she frantically threw the rock. It was such a weak toss, though, that it only flew a couple of feet before flopping to the ground. There was silence. Then there was the sound of laughter reverberating against the trees. Whatever tension Cassidy and I had started to build, magically disappeared the moment we witnessed Winnie's pathetic display of athletics. "What was *that?*" Cassidy asked with a laugh.

Winnie, the only one not finding the humor, tried to defend herself. "She told me to throw the rock. I threw the rock!"

"Okay, okay," I said, regaining my composure, "let's start over." I retrieved another rock from the bank of the stream and handed it to her. "This time, when you throw it, I want you to throw the rock really hard and yell out your frustration. Got it?"

"Okay," Winnie acknowledged hesitantly. When she threw the rock the second time, it went much farther, which was an improvement. However, her declaration was said weakly and without conviction. I could just barely hear the words "mean people."

I wanted to cringe, but in an attempt to be encouraging, I said, "Okay, that was better, but this time I want you to *really* yell it. Nobody's going to hear you out here, so let it out." Realizing that getting her to loosen up was going to be a process, I grabbed a whole handful of stones this time.

Her second attempt was a little louder, but not great. Maybe what she needed was an example. "YO, CASSIDY," I shouted, tossing her a stone, "you're the president of the Public Speaking Club. Show this girl how to be heard all the way in the back of a crowded auditorium."

"What should I yell?" she asked.

"Whatever it is that frustrates you. Get crazy, go nuts!"

She thought for a minute before a mischievous smirk crossed her face. Winding up her arm like a softball player, she threw the rock and screamed, "FREEZING IN THE WOODS WITH A CRAZY GIRL!"

"Wow . . . that was cold, Cassidy."

"I thought you'd like that," she said with a grin, clearly proud of herself. I had to admit, I liked her style.

"Okay, watch and learn, Funny Bones. I'll show you how it's really done." Keeping three rocks, I gave the rest to Cassidy. Throwing the first one with gusto, I screamed, "BOARDING SCHOOLS!" Immediately, I threw the second yelling, "ROOMMATES!" With the third rock I shouted, "TINY, SASSY, GINGER GIRLS!"

After that, it was on! The evening turned into a frenzy of stone throwing and shouting. Some declarations were serious, some were funny, and others were said through so much laughter I couldn't tell what they were! Winnie joined in on the fun, voicing her frustrations with footballs, bad stain remover, and people who tell her to "speak up." Ironically, she said the last one so loud I think she might have scared a bird! It felt good to finally see her letting loose.

It also felt good to let go of some of my own frustrations. I'd built up a lot over the last couple of years, and although I certainly didn't voice them all, for those few precious moments it was as if all my problems were washed downstream.

Finally exhausted, we sat down for a few moments on the cool ground to catch our breath. Cassidy, unsurprisingly, was the first to find her voice and asked, "Ava, how did you find this place anyway?"

"Uh, what?" I'd heard her, I just wasn't sure how I wanted to respond.

"How did you find this place? You've only been here a day."

"There are satellite images of this place on the internet. If you zoom in, you can see the stream in the photos."

"Why were you looking at satellite images?"

There it was: the question I didn't really want to answer. I had a feeling the explanation might make me look a little unstable. Not wanting to lie to them, though, I decided to fess up. "Well, when I was told I was being sent here . . . I kind of . . . planned an alternative method of leaving." *There, that sounded on the up-and-up.*

"You planned an escape route?!"

Rats. Leave it to Cassidy to make it sound like I was attempting to bust out of Sing Sing. "Look, in my defense, I was very upset about being sent here and I didn't know what it was going to be like."

"But you're not going to run away now, are you?" Winnie asked sweetly.

"Yeah," Cassidy chimed in, "Now that you know how wonderful we all are! I mean, where else are you going to find two girls *clearly* as nuts as you are?" She made a gesture prompting me to take a look at where we were sitting.

I chuckled, "Well then, I guess I don't really have a choice. I'll have to stay." It had been a long time since I'd had a real friend. I didn't want to get my hopes up, but it now looked as if I might have two.

When the cold became too much for us to bear, we headed back inside and waved goodnight. I was in a great mood—until I opened my door, that is. Maci was sitting in her desk chair, legs crossed and eyes narrowed, waiting for me. "Where is it?" she demanded.

"Where is what?"

"You know what."

I sighed, "No Maci, I don't." Aside from the fact that I really had no idea what she was talking about, I was tired and just wanted to go to sleep. My luggage had been delivered to the room and the bag I knew contained my pajamas was sitting on the bed. As I walked toward it, however, Maci stood up and aggressively blocked my path.

"Where's my necklace you klepto little freak?"

"*Excuse me?*" I asked, shocked by the sudden hostility.

"You heard me! I had a Tiffany necklace worth over $2,500 that my Daddy gave to me, sitting on my nightstand. Now, suddenly, it's gone!"

"And you think *I* took it?"

"Good guess, Nancy Drew!"

"Okay, you need to chill out," I told her, trying to diffuse the situation despite my rising irritation. "I didn't take your ridiculously priced necklace. In fact, please allow me to go on record as saying that I am not *at all* interested in *any* of your stuff!"

"Then where is it?"

"How should I know?!"

Counting on her fingers, she began to map out her case against me. "You were the only person left alone in the room with my necklace, you're a criminal, and now it's gone. Gee, what conclusion can we deduce from that, Nancy Drew?"

In an act of retaliation, I made a show of counting on my fingers as I said, "That you've misplaced your necklace, we're not gonna be 'besties,' and that Nancy Drew's the only mystery book you've ever read."

Her eyes narrowed. "Oh, look who thinks they're clever. Well let me tell you something Jailbird, you'd better return my necklace or . . ."

"Or *what?*"

A slow, malicious smile spread across her face. Stepping closer to me, she raised herself to her full height and stared me directly in the eyes. In a voice that was calm, but threatening, she said, "I'm not a person you want to tangle with."

If there was one thing I wasn't going to let her do, it was threaten me. I squared my shoulders and stared right back at her. "I'm not afraid of you."

"Oh really?"

"Really." The silence was palpable. Ready to end the showdown, I said, "Now, if you'll excuse me, I'm going to bed. I'm tired of this conversation." I walked around her and she allowed me to pass. While I was grabbing my pajamas, I could sense her eyes practically burning a hole in the back of my head. I simply ignored her as I proceeded to get ready for bed. Although the fight had ended for the night, I wasn't stupid enough to believe it was really over. As I turned out the lights and allowed the weight of the day to pull my eyes shut, I wondered to myself: *Is it physically possible to sleep with one eye open?*

5

AVA

I struggled to get up the next morning, knowing that my first day of school awaited me. The experience was almost exactly what I expected it would be. I got lost trying to find some of my classes, had to sit through a bunch of boring lectures, and nobody talked to me except Cassidy and Winnie. Just to add insult to injury, the History teacher publicly shamed me for falling asleep during his speech on some random person that died, like, a thousand years ago.

At lunch, Winnie refused to eat in the cafeteria, so Cassidy and I bought chips and cold sandwiches from the school's general store and ate with her out on the front lawn. It was a bit cooler outside than I would have liked, but there wasn't any way she was going to face the crowd again so soon. Cassidy had told me in confidence that pictures of the incident were being passed around online. So far, Winnie had kept to herself and stayed off her phone, so we were hoping she hadn't seen them yet. What a relief it was that she was more interested in reading books than she was in reading internet gossip!

Cassidy took a bite of her sandwich. "So," she mumbled with her mouth full, "wuff wif da looks Maffi keefs givin' you?"

"What?" I asked.

Cassidy swallowed, "What's with the looks Maci keeps giving you? I noticed her 'anger meter' is cranked all the way up today. What gives?"

"She thinks I stole her necklace."

"Did you?"

"NO!"

"Sorry, just asking," she said defensively. Hurriedly, she added, "I mean, I didn't really think you took her necklace, but I thought I should ask. I don't know why you'd take it. It's not really your style. Not to say that necklaces aren't your style, they could be your style. We haven't known each other that long . . ."

"CASSIDY!"

"What?"

"You're babbling."

"Sorry."

Note to self: Don't make Cassidy nervous. "It's fine," I said, "I get why you'd ask, but I didn't take it and now Maci's out for blood."

"Want me to talk to her?"

"NO," I said a little too quickly. "I mean, no thank you. I'm capable of fighting my own battles." In a show of strength I added, "Besides, I think I can handle one little prissy princess. Like, what's she gonna do? Toss a tiara at my head?"

There are questions in life that should never be asked. For instance, questions like, "What's she gonna do?" are almost always followed by something terrible and unexpected. I should have known this. I'd watched enough movies. Yet, somehow, I was still surprised when I walked into my room later that evening and discovered that all my stuff was gone! It wasn't just my clothes and knickknacks that were gone, no, *everything* was gone. My bed, my desk, my chair, everything had vanished like one giant Houdini illusion. My mouth fell open in utter shock.

Hearing the door click, I turned around and found Maci standing there, looking as coy as the Cheshire Cat. Struggling to snap out of my stupor, I eventually managed to ask, "Where's my stuff?"

"Huh," Maci began, as she arrogantly strode into the room, "seems like I asked you the same question yesterday. Funny how the tables have turned."

"Maci, give me back my stuff." I was trying to keep my words steady, though my anger boiled inside me and threatened to explode all over the room.

"No," she said simply.

"Maci, give me back my stuff or else I'll tell . . ."

"Who? The headmaster? And tell her what? That *I* had something to do with it? It'll be your word against mine. *I'm* an upstanding student with powerful connections. *You're* a newbie with a rap sheet. Face it, for all she knows you're just a pathetic little loser, who did all this to yourself in some desperate attempt to get someone to notice her." Her lips curled into an artificial pout as she mockingly added, "So sad." Eyes twinkling, she chuckled wickedly. This girl was gaining way too much pleasure out of hurting me.

I wish I could say I wasn't bothered by it, but parts of what she'd said had hit a nerve. I wanted to cry, but there was no way I was going to give her the satisfaction. "Give it back," I demanded. My voice contained a slight tremble that I hoped didn't give away my true emotions.

"I don't have your stuff. . . . Honest!"

"Then who does?"

A slight smile tugged at the corners of her lips, "Dr. Keller."

I wasn't sure how to respond. Of all the names I'd expected to hear, "Keller" wasn't in the top 10. Heck, that name wasn't in the top 1,000! Maci sauntered over to the window, looked out, and then knowingly looked back at me. Scowling, I strode over to see what she was looking at. There was nothing outside—at least nothing out of the ordinary. I couldn't figure it out. Then it hit me. "You put my stuff in *there*?!"

Smiling she said, "Well, I know you're not afraid of *me*. Can you honestly say the same about him?"

I took another look out the window at the so-called "haunted" building. It was getting dark and, as if on cue, I heard the rolling sound of thunder and the pitter patter of raindrops. It didn't matter that I didn't believe in ghosts, that building was the last place I wanted to be at night.

"You'd better get going," Maci said with artificial sweetness, "I hear there's a chance of rain."

By the time I reached the old science building, the rain was coming down hard. Maci hadn't been kind enough to leave me an umbrella, so I was forced to accept the drenching. The only good part about the rain was that it disguised my tears. Internally, I berated myself for being so weak.

As I reached the front steps, I heard the sound of feet hurriedly splashing behind me. "WHAT DO YOU THINK YOU'RE DOING?" Cassidy yelled through the storm. "ARE YOU TRYING TO GET SICK?"

"WHAT ARE YOU GUYS DOING HERE?" I yelled back.

"We followed you," Winnie explained through chattering teeth. A clap of thunder struck, which caused her to jump and hide herself behind Cassidy. I swear, that girl was more like a "Piglet" than a "Winnie." All it took to scare her was a blustery day.

"We were sitting in the lounge," Cassidy explained further, "and saw you storming out the front door without an umbrella. Here . . ."

She'd brought with her a second umbrella, which she handed to me. It was a sweet gesture, but a little pointless now that I'd already been soaked. I opened it anyway. "So now can you please tell us what it is you're doing out here?" she asked.

"I'm getting my stuff back."

"What?"

"Maci took all my stuff and put it in there," I pointed to the entrance whose locks had been broken by, I was assuming, a pair of bolt cutters. "I'm getting it back!"

"Why didn't you tell us? This is stupid! Just stay in our room tonight and get out of the rain!" The offer sounded tempting, and was probably the most sensible solution, but once again, I'd committed to my mission. I wasn't afraid of Maci, or the ghost of Dr. Keller, or anyone else and I certainly wasn't going to let that vindictive viper of a roommate get the better of me!

"Thanks, but I don't need help. I can handle Maci on my own."

"Oh really? How's that working out for you?"

Her words only heightened my determination. I lowered the umbrella she'd given me and shoved it toward her. "I'm fine!" With that, I ran up the sloping stone steps, unwound the broken chain from the handles, and stepped inside.

As the door slammed shut behind me, the building's brick walls muffled the sound of the rain, turning it into a hollow reminder of the outside world. "*Whoa*," I whispered as I scanned the room. Although Cassidy had said the building was closed in the 1970's, I was certain it had been built long before then.

On my right was a grand staircase, showcasing a banister carved out of dark-mahogany wood that dramatically cascaded down from the second floor and curved into the shape of a griffin. On my left, was a wide hallway leading to the back of the building. It was there, that a large gothic-style window was suddenly illuminated by a flash of lightning. As grand as the building once was, its beauty was now offset by debris covering the floor, paint that was peeling off the walls, and chains dangling from the ceiling that had, at one point in time, held light fixtures. One of the walls was spray painted in graffiti that read:

JB ♥ CL

I didn't know who "JB" or "CL" were, or why they found vandalism romantic, but I wished they had just bought a valentine like everyone else.

Although the building was somewhat creepy, falling apart, and smelled like mildew; there was still something special about it. Looking around, I tried to imagine what it had been like when it was new. In my mind, I envisioned school children laughing with each other in the hallway, racing up the stairs to class, tapping me on the . . . *wait* . . . *that was real!* Screaming, I whipped around and punched at whoever was behind me. Also screaming, Cassidy and Winnie just barely avoided getting hit by my fist.

"Geez-o-peat!" I yelled. "You two almost gave me a heart attack!"

"And you almost smashed in our faces," Cassidy bit back. "I think we're even."

"Why are you here? I thought I told you I was fine."

"We talked it over and decided that we weren't going to let you do this alone," she said, trying to exude bravery. But her shaky tone and bulging eyes told a different story. She added, "Even if we get haunted and never ever come out, we want to help you."

"I want to go back to the dorm," Winnie whispered. Cassidy smacked her on the arm.

35

"You don't have to do this," I said.

"Yes, we do," Cassidy replied with a little more confidence in her voice.

I knew how scared they both were, so I couldn't help but be a little touched at their willingness to join me. "Fine, you can come," I declared. Cassidy looked a little pleased, but Winnie just looked like she wanted to throw up.

"So," Cassidy said, looking around the room, "where do you think it is?"

6

CASSIDY

'*Courage is not the absence of fear* . . .' *How did that quote go again? Something like, 'but just* . . . *the act of sucking it up and doing it anyway.' No, that's not right. Whatever, close enough!* For the past 15 minutes, I'd been reciting encouraging quotes to myself in the hopes that they would stop me from completely freaking out. For four years, I'd successfully avoided going anywhere near the old science building. Now, thanks to the (possibly misguided) feeling of moral obligation to help a friend, I was getting the grand tour of "Ghost Land."

We'd been following our guide, Ava, around for what seemed like an eternity; and I was getting increasingly irritated with her. We searched room after room, using our phones as flashlights. And room after room, we found nothing. Yet, instead of leaving right away, Ava would stand around taking her good sweet time, just staring at the ruins. I mean, if this was how slow she was looking at rooms full of *nothing*, I'd hate to see how slow she'd be at a museum!

A mouse scuttled across the floor, causing Winnie to scream and dig her nails into my arm. "OWWW! Declaw yourself, woman!" I scolded her, smacking the back of her hand. In an attempt to hurry Ava along, I asked,

"So, Maci didn't say anything about where she hid your stuff? No clue? Nothing at all?"

"No," Ava said, aimlessly scanning yet another empty room. "She just said it was 'with Dr. Keller,' whatever that means."

I couldn't believe it. Here we'd been walking around aimlessly this whole time and she hadn't bothered to mention this crucial piece of information. "Isn't it obvious?" I asked with a sigh. "If it's 'with Dr. Keller,' then I'm guessing it's where he spent most of his time. His office."

We may not have known exactly where his office was, but by using reasonable deductions and the process of elimination, it wasn't long before we found a door labeled, "Dr. Laurence Keller, Ph.D." Just reading his name made my stomach churn uncomfortably and my palms start to sweat. I really didn't want to go in, but I also wanted our little journey down dead-people's memory lane to come to an end.

Looking over at Ava, I noticed that she, too, seemed a bit more uncomfortable than she had been a moment ago. "After you," I said with a grand gesture toward the door. Giving me a look out of the corner of her eye, she wiped her hand on her skirt and turned the handle. Nothing.

"Well, go on Braveheart, turn the handle," I said.

"I'm trying," she replied, pushing on the solid-wood door with her shoulder.

"I think it's locked," Winnie whispered.

Rolling her eyes, Ava said, "Thanks Winnie, I picked up on that." She glared angrily at the door for a few minutes before turning to look at me. With a heavy sigh, she held out her hand. "Give me your hair pins."

"Why?" I asked.

Rolling her eyes again, she repeated, "Give me your hair pins."

With a sinking suspicion of what she was about to do, I took out a few of my bobby pins, which varied in size, and handed them over to her. My hair required a lot of metal to keep it together. With the removal of just a few pins, the dam broke, causing my mess of curls to erupt like a geyser.

Ava assessed what I'd given her, picked out the ones she wanted to use, bent them a little, and inserted them into the skeleton keyhole. *Yep, that was what I was afraid she was going to do.* I spent the next few seconds internally debating whether or not I should ask her how she knew about lock picking. Then I heard a *click*.

Turning to me with steely dark eyes, she handed my pins back and said, "Don't ask."

I guess that answers that.

Once open, the door announced our entrance with a loud *screech*. Cautiously, we stepped inside. Now, I may not have been impressed by the plaster-covered floors and empty cabinetry that adorned the other rooms, but Dr. Keller's office was different. Nothing inside had been touched!

"Groovy," I said as I looked around the room. Aside from the desk, which was a very large, ornate, wood monstrosity; the rest of the office was a glorified time capsule of the 1970's. Atop the desk was a yellow landline telephone, grey electric typewriter, and some kind of rotating device that held index cards with people's names on them. The brown vinyl chair behind the desk looked pretty comfy, but the dust and mouse-chewed holes reminded me I should probably stay standing. The left side of the room featured an orange, vinyl sofa; orange, mouse-chewed, shag rug; and a large bookshelf that displayed both books and science stuff. Although I was hoping not to see the ghost of Dr. Keller, I wondered if he'd haunt me less if I told him how much I liked his style.

Looking down at the desk, I picked up a framed photograph. The man in the picture didn't look anything like the Dr. Keller I'd envisioned. I pictured an old guy with a white moustache and frizzy hair. You know, kind of like Einstein, but with "crazy eyes." Instead, the Dr. Keller I was looking at was young and handsome. He had brown hair, a wide smile, and kind eyes that were accentuated by his large wire-rimmed glasses. Both he and the woman he was standing next to wore white lab coats. I took a closer look at the woman. She was wearing glasses, a turtleneck sweater, and her brown hair was pulled up into a ponytail. Were they co-workers or were they more than that? I'd never thought of Providence's ghost as having a girlfriend. *Nah*, I thought, setting the picture down, *she looks much too serious for him.*

"Oh look, filing cabinets," Ava said angrily, as she pulled open a closet door. Slamming it shut she asked, "Where's my stuff Cassidy?"

"How should I know?"

"You said it would be in ghost-boy's office. You said it was *obvious*. Well, where is it?"

"What's eating you?" I asked, completely shocked by Ava's sudden mood change.

"None of your business!"

I felt my eyes bulge out of my head. "*None* of my business? None of my business?! I risked life and limb to follow Your Highness, Queen of Stubbornness, into this building. I didn't have to! If it was up to me, I'd be eating popcorn and watching a movie right about now!"

"So go," she commanded, verbally stabbing me in the chest. "I told you not to come."

That was the last straw. "Fine," I said simply. "Come on Winnie, we're leaving." I had no idea what had possessed Ava to turn into such a jerk, but I certainly wasn't going to stand around while she took her problems out on me.

Winnie looked emotionally conflicted, but followed my lead. Just as I reached the door, however, it closed. Nobody had touched it, there was no wind, and yet . . . it had closed. Frantically, I pulled on the knob. It wouldn't budge.

"What's happening?!" Winnie cried. A bolt of thunder clapped. Rain beat against the window. But the sound that really scared me, was the sound of a train. Screaming, Winnie dove under the desk.

Oh my goodness, this is it, I thought. This was the moment I'd been dreading. Dr. Keller's ghost was coming for us! I wanted to run, but the only part of my body that was racing was my heart. My feet were frozen to the ground and my knees threatened to give way. I couldn't breathe. All I could do was stare at the door and hope that he wouldn't be able to see me. *Oh who are you kidding, Cassidy? You have bright red hair, and he has glasses the size of the Hubble telescope. He'll see you!*

"Wait a minute," I heard Ava whisper, "do you hear that?"

At first, all I could hear was my own heartbeat. But then I heard it, too. It was faint, but it sounded like . . . snickering. Ava quickly strode towards the door and flung it open. Standing in the doorway was Nolan, Victor, and David: The Three Stooges. They stumbled a little, previously having had their ears pressed up against the door. Upon seeing my face, their stifled giggles turned into full-on laughter. I felt my face flush in anger. Not thinking clearly, I screamed, "LET ME AT 'EM!" and launched myself at whichever one got in my way.

"Whoa there, Sparky," Ava said as she grabbed me around the waist. My legs flung wildly in the air, but were too short to kick anybody. The boys laughed even harder. After Ava set me down, I took a moment to get control of my anger. "You . . . *you* . . ." I seethed.

Temporarily having a better command over her vocabulary, Ava took control of the situation and asked, "What on earth are you guys doing here?"

"Scaring you," Victor said with a laugh.

"Tessa told me that she and Maci were planning on playing a little practical joke on you," Nolan added. "So, we thought we'd make it a bit more memorable."

"YOU SCARED THE LIVING DAYLIGHTS OUT OF ME, NOLAN!" I screamed.

"Oh, come on, don't be a big baby! You were never in any real danger. Personally, I thought we were quite clever." He held up a clear string with a bent paper clip tied to the end. "We hooked a fishing line to the door handle to pull it shut, then held it closed when you tried to open it. Simple, crude, but effective."

"And the train noise?" I asked, less than impressed with their antics. David held up his phone and pressed a button. The sound of a train blared through the speakers.

"Okay, ha-ha," Ava said sarcastically, "you've all had your fun. Now be gone, all of you." She swished her hands at them, but the boys held their ground.

"Oh, come on, don't be like that," Nolan said to her. "We were just having some fun."

"And now you've had it. Shoo-shoo!" She flicked her hands at them again.

Nolan smiled, "Look, maybe we got off on the wrong foot."

"Seems to me, that's the only kind you've got."

"Then let me prove you wrong. We'll stay and help you get your stuff back."

"We will?" David asked with a gulp.

"Of course we will," said Nolan authoritatively. "We're always available to help a few damsels in distress."

Yuck!

"Funny," Ava said, "the only distress we've had today was when you clowns showed up."

"I don't believe you."

"I don't really care what you believe."

Watching Ava and Nolan bicker was like watching a ping pong match. My eyes kept darting back-and-forth waiting for someone to drop the ball.

Nolan paused for a moment and then asked, "Well, what if I told you I knew exactly where they put your stuff?"

BOOM! Point for Nolan.

Ava bit her lip as she tried to decide how to respond. I didn't know what on earth she was waiting for! Answering for her, I yelled, "Deal! Where is it?"

"CASSIDY," Ava screamed, as if I'd just betrayed her.

"Ava, enough! I'm as angry at them as you are, but believe it or not, I'd like to get out of here sometime this century. We need to focus on getting your stuff, getting to the dorm, and going to bed. If that requires putting up with three egg-heads to do it, then I say let's make a flippin' omelet!"

"Thanks Cassidy," Nolan said inauthentically, "you have always had a way with words."

"Fine," Ava relented. "Where'd they put it?"

Nolan crossed his arms and tilted his chin up, clearly enjoying his newfound power, "In Dr. Keller's private lab, of course."

All the fear I had let go of came rushing back with a vengeance. "In the basement?" I managed to squeak out. Over the years, I'd heard stories about the underground lab and the horrifying experiments that had taken place. It hadn't occurred to me to suggest looking there because I didn't figure anyone would be crazy enough to go down there. I had underestimated Maci.

"Fine, let's go," Ava said casually. Clearly, she didn't fully grasp the magnitude of the situation. "Where's Winnie?"

Oops! I had been so focused on my own fears that I'd completely forgotten about the most fearful of us all. I walked around the desk, fully expecting to find her crouched underneath it, cowering in the fetal position. Instead, I found her crouched underneath it, reading a book! "Winnie, what are you doing?"

"I'm reading."

"Well, I can see that!" Offering her my hand, I helped pull her out from underneath the desk. "What I don't understand, is how you always manage to find a book."

"I didn't find it, it found me. When I hid under the desk, I must have hit something, because a panel moved and smacked me in the head. When I took a look inside, there were all these books."

Bending over, I peered under the desk. Everything looked normal to me. "Are you sure?" I asked her.

"Of course I am," she insisted. "Hit the right side."

I bent over again and pressed the right panel. Sure enough, it swung open. Inside the hidden compartment were about 11 thin, leather-bound books. I pulled one out and read the cover aloud, "*The Lightning Sphere Reports by Dr. Laurence Keller Ph.D.* They sure do like to add the 'Ph.D.' don't they?"

"What's it about?" Ava asked as she took the book out of my hands and started flipping through the pages. *Rude!* I picked up another one and opened it up. It was handwritten like a diary, with dates and locations at the top of each page.

"As far as I can tell," Winnie answered, "he's written stories about history."

"What?" I asked in surprise. "That seems like an odd choice for a science teacher. If it were me, I'd be writing about my cool experiments or different theories I had."

"You would," Victor mumbled.

"And what's a 'lightning sphere?'"

Winnie shrugged her shoulders. "I don't know. I haven't found where he explains any of that."

"What a waste!" Victor said, as he grabbed the book out of my hands. *Double rude!* "The guy had a hidden compartment under his desk and he used it to store books. What a nerd!"

"And what would you use it for?" I asked.

With a smirk, he replied, "Wouldn't you like to know?"

"He'd use it to hide junk food," David spoke up. "Trust me, I've seen this guy put away an entire box of donuts. By *himself!*" Victor smacked David on the shoulder with the book. He didn't do it hard, but David still yelled, "Ow!"

"Is book club about over?" Nolan asked impatiently.

"I'm ready when you are," Ava replied, tossing her book on the desk.

"Then let's go folks! Time is money, and mine's expensive!"

As we followed him out of the office, I noticed that Winnie was starting to leave with one of the books. Pulling her aside, I whispered through gritted teeth, "What do you think you're doing?"

"What?" she asked innocently. I silently pointed to the book in her arms. "I'm not done reading."

"So you're gonna steal it?!"

"I'm not stealing, just borrowing. I'll bring it back. Or . . ." she hesitated, looking around the room, "get Ava to bring it back."

"This isn't a library, Winnie."

"Of course it isn't! Libraries are beautiful places that protect and share books. This place is horrible! The books here are left abandoned, with no other purpose than to disintegrate or get eaten by a rat. I'm doing it a favor!"

How could I argue with a person who talked about books as if they were people? "Fine," I mumbled reluctantly. "But if the ghost of Dr. Keller comes back for his book, you're on your own!"

7

AVA

Compared to the basement, the rest of the building looked as lovely as the Ritz Carlton. Not built for looks, the underground world we now found ourselves in made no effort to cover its brick walls or hide its web of piping. Feeling right at home, the spiders decorated the space with their unique form of drapery.

Highlighting our silence was the rhythmic *plop* of a water leak and the *crunch* of broken glass beneath our feet. With only the flashlights on our cell phones to light our path, my concern was less about what I could see and more about what I couldn't. Pulling my shirt up over my nose in a futile attempt to keep the mold spores out of my lungs, I silently wondered: *Why would the head of the science department, a guy with influence, choose such a depressing place to put his lab?* The only answer I could come up with was that he had wanted to hide whatever it was he'd been working on. It wasn't a comforting thought.

"We're here!" Nolan announced. The metal chains, that had held the battered-wooden door closed, were lying on the ground in a heap.

Picking them up, I examined the end. "Bolt cutters," I concluded and tossed them to the side. "I can see Maci's fingerprints are all over this place."

Any cautious voice in my head was muffled by the anger I felt toward Maci. Without hesitation, I flung open the door and waltzed right in. Wooden shelving lined the walls displaying dusty beakers, jars of various liquids, and disassembled pieces of electronic equipment.

In the center of the room, standing-height work tables were covered with microscopes and sharp tools. What the room didn't have, however, was my stuff.

Whipping around, I screamed, "NOLAN, THIS ISN'T FUNNY!"

"My, my, you're an angry little person, aren't you?" he quipped.

Yes indeed, I was an angry person. I was a very angry person. I was being harassed by my roommate, mocked by an arrogant preppy, made to look like a criminal in front of my friends, and was spending the evening traipsing around the lair of a psycho scientist. If anyone had a reason to be angry, it was me!

"Now, don't get your knee-highs in a twist," Nolan continued, "Tessa said they put it all in a back room." He led me over to a door at the far end of the lab.

The room inside was very strange. Large cushions were affixed to the walls and, above my head, metal wiring was woven in a web-like manner across the ceiling. I had no idea what the purpose of such a room would be, but I was positive I didn't want to know. In the center were all my things, just as Nolan had said. Maci had set them up as if this room were just a normal bedroom. She'd made my bed, decorated my desk, and hung my clothes on the ceiling wires. Lying on the bed, was a note. Walking over, I picked it up. It read:

Welcome to Providence, Ava!
Finally, we found a room that suits you.
Enjoy your padded cell!

My face felt hot. Crumpling the note in my hand, I threw it on the floor. She was driving me to my breaking point and, in terms of the school year, I was only on day two!

Nolan picked up the crumpled note. "So," he began cautiously, after he'd finished reading it, "I've been trying to figure out what it is you did to land yourself on Providence's Most Wanted list. After reading this note, it's become crystal clear—you're a sugar addict! That's right, I've found you out! You consume all you can in a single sitting, and then start bouncing off the walls. Hide your cookies Grandma, lock up your lollipops little Timmy, Ava the Sweet Snatcher is in town!" Though Nolan was trying to lighten the mood, he had failed miserably. "Nothing? Not even a smirk?"

"I'm in no mood, Nolan," I said dryly.

"Wanna talk about it?"

"Not really."

"Oh, come on!" he insisted, plopping himself down in my office chair. "To my friends, I'm practically a psychologist."

"We're not friends."

Impersonating seriousness he asked, "And how does that make you feel?"

I'd had enough of his games. Turning, I left to find someone—anyone else—who could help me carry out my stuff.

Back in the lab, Victor hefted a circular object out of a solid metal box and lobbed it at David with a shout of, "GO LONG!" Previously busy examining a microscope, David caught the ball at the expense of his phone and the microscope—both of which clattered to the ground.

"Stop touching things!" Cassidy screamed from the entryway.

"Why?" Victor asked, motioning to David to throw the ball back. "Are you afraid you'll make Dr. Keller mad? I hear he's got a really bad temper."

"Stop it, Victor!" Cassidy's voice shook a little as she tried to control the situation. "You don't know what any of this stuff does. For all we know, that ball could be dangerous!" It didn't immediately strike me as something that would be dangerous, just heavy. It looked to be made out of a polished, silver metal and had a raised, gold band wrapped around the middle.

"Scary things from the 70's," Victor replied dismissively, "I'll make sure to add this ball on the list, right next to car phones and bellbottoms."

"Victor, I'm serious!"

Ready to end the bickering, I interrupted, "Hey, Victor! Can you help me grab some of my stuff?"

"Sure thing," he said, tossing the ball not to David, but to Cassidy. Winnie was clinging to one of her arms, yet she somehow still managed to catch it right before it hit the ground. But as soon as it touched her hands, a *crack* of lightning erupted outside. Screams were heard as the lights on our phones flickered and went out.

ERIN C.J. HANEY

"Hey, who turned out the lights?" came Nolan's voice from somewhere behind me.

Whirring and snapping sounds filled the room. I recognized Cassidy's scream, which was followed by a *thud*. A mere second later, the room glowed in a bright blue light. Its origin was a pulsing blue circle in the center of the floor. Hovering above the circle was the silver ball. The two ends, separated by the golden band, were spinning frantically in opposite directions.

"WHAT DID YOU DO?! " Victor screamed at Cassidy.

"ME?! I DIDN'T . . ." The rest of her sentence was drowned out by the sound of rushing wind.

The blue light on the floor grew bigger and bigger. I felt my body being sucked toward its core. I tried to run, but it was too fast. Before I knew it, my feet were sinking beneath me. In desperation, I grabbed the leg of one of the work tables. The rusted bolts holding it to the floor rattled, threatening to give way. A hand grabbed my foot. I figured it was one of my friends, but I didn't look back to see who. I was concentrating solely on not letting go.

Sweat seeped from my palms, my fingers burned, then I slipped. No longer able to hold on, I fell into the void. Looking up, a circular picture of the world I knew grew smaller and smaller until it was gone. My vision grew dark. The last sound I heard, was the roaring of a train.

8

AVA

Warm light pushed against my eyelids, prompting them to open with a heavy reluctance. I found myself staring at a bright, open sky framed by tree branches. A large bird streaked across it, as if all was right with the world. But I knew better. This wasn't right. I wasn't supposed to be there. I felt the sharp pain of a rock digging into my back and the foliage I was lying on was beginning to itch. Slowly regaining my senses, I lifted myself up. Dizziness set in and I quickly closed my eyes. *Where am I?*

Though my head was foggy, I tried to think back to the last thing I remembered. *I was in a dark lab . . . there was a blue circle . . . I was falling.* As the memories flooded in, so did the panic. Scrambling up off the ground, I frantically looked around. Though I was in the middle of a forest; beakers, boxes, and tools were strewn all over the ground. So were my friends.

"Winnie!" I screamed as I ran over to her. The poor thing was flopped over in a shrub. To my relief, her eyes started to open.

"Where am I?" she mumbled.

"Your guess is as good as mine," I replied, ungracefully lifting her onto her feet.

"Why am I in the woods?" she pitifully asked, trying to focus her eyes. "I don't wanna be in the woods."

"That makes two of us." Certain that she was going to be okay, I turned my attention to the others. They had all slowly gotten up and were each mentally in their own worlds. Cassidy was picking leaves out of her hair, Nolan was digging through the wreckage, Victor was desperately trying to get his phone to work, and David . . . where was David? The snap of a large tree branch, a scream, and a *thud* answered my question. Dazed, but seemingly okay, David stood up and adjusted his glasses.

"What just happened?" he asked, eyes darting wildly about.

"Don't know," Victor briskly replied, not even bothering to look at him. His entire focus was zeroed in on whatever buttons he was pressing on his phone. "David, where's your phone?"

"*That's* your question?" he replied indignantly.

"I'm not getting any signal and mine's almost dead."

Scowling, David started rummaging around the debris, muttering, " 'Are you okay, David?' 'Sorry you fell from a tree, David.' How about a simple, 'Glad to see you're not DEAD, David!'" Finally, he found what he was looking for. "Here Victor, catch!" He tossed the phone over to his friend.

"It's broken!" Victor exclaimed.

"Better it than me!"

Their bickering was drowned out by shouting coming from Cassidy and Nolan. "PUT IT DOWN, NOLAN!" Cassidy screamed, scrambling to her feet.

"NO WAY!" Nolan shouted back. "We need it!" He had picked up the metal ball and was holding it tightly to his chest; on the off-chance that she would attempt to take it away by force.

It proved an unnecessary measure since, instead of moving toward him, she took a few steps back. "It's not safe!"

"How do you know?"

"Yeah," Victor chimed in, pointing an accusatory finger in her direction. "What button did you push to get us sent here?"

"I didn't push anything! I have no idea what happened! All I know is that I wasn't standing HERE before that shiny thing started spinning like . . ." Frantically flopping her hands around in the air, she tried to demonstrate the spinning motion, but ended up looking like . . . well . . . I'm not sure what she looked like, but it was weird.

David turned on Victor, "The only reason that ball was even able to send us here is because you started throwing it!"

"Hey, don't look at me!" Victor shot back. "It wasn't doing anything weird until Cassidy touched it."

"Cassidy, touch it," Nolan commanded, throwing the ball for her to catch. Instead, she screamed and dove out of the way.

"Come on! How do you think we're going to get back? By clicking our heels three times and saying, 'there's no place like home?' If this ball sent us here, then we need to get it to send us back!"

Victor marched over to the ball. "I'll get it to work." With an open palm, he gave it several hard whacks.

David's eyes bulged. "You're going to get it to work by *smacking* it?!"

"That's how you fix electronics, duh!"

Everyone's shouting began to overlap, swirling together with Winnie's whimpering, to create a cacophony as painful as nails on a chalkboard. "STOP IT!" I screamed, instantly giving the forest back its serenity. All eyes were on me. Stepping toward them, I continued, "Fighting isn't going to solve anything. Now, I don't know where we are or how we got here, but we aren't going to answer any of our questions by standing in the middle of the woods. I say we try to calm down and think this through like rational people."

Victor glared at me, "Who died and made you queen?"

"I'm sorry Victor, do you have a problem with *thinking*?"

He opened his mouth, but when no retort came out, he quickly sealed his lips.

"Good," I continued. "First of all, David, we're all glad you're okay."

"Thank you," he acknowledged with a nod and a side-eye to Victor.

"Now Victor," I said, ignoring his glare, "are you getting any cell phone signal at all?"

With a smirk he answered, "Yes, that's why I'm not calling anyone."

Smart aleck. "Well, maybe it's your phone. Has anyone else tried their phone?" Nolan and Winnie weren't sure where theirs had landed and Cassidy's was dead. Fishing mine out of my pocket, I handed it to him. "Try this."

Victor took it without a word and started walking from tree to tree, waving the phone in the air, trying to get a signal.

The rest of us took a seat on the hard ground. Cassidy made sure to sit a safe distance away from Nolan and the ball, yet her eyes remained trained on the mysterious object. Quietly lying on the grass, it was unrecognizable from the spinning, snapping contraption we had seen in the lab. "This is bad," Cassidy murmured after about 10 minutes had passed. "This is very, very bad. Victor should be getting a signal. Why isn't he getting a signal?"

Clearly annoyed, Nolan dropped his head against a tree and sighed, "Relax would ya? We're in the woods. It's not as if they put cell phone towers up everywhere. Haven't you ever been camping?"

A strange look momentarily crossed her face before she blurted out, "But you typically *go* camping. You don't *wake up* camping. I'm telling you, there's something about this that's really off, really weird, really bad!"

"What gave it away?" David grumbled. "The spinning blue orb of doom?"

"I mean more than that!" Cassidy was really getting herself worked up. She was like a top that was about to spin right off a table. "There's something else! There something . . . *more.* I just can't put my finger on it."

"And what are you basing that on?" Nolan asked. "Your brilliant intuition?"

Cassidy glared at him. "Fine, don't believe me. I'm used to it. But when you find out I'm right, just remember—I told you so!"

Nolan scoffed and rolled his eyes. He was so arrogant that I momentarily hoped Cassidy would get the last laugh. Then I remembered how she'd said there was something "really bad" about this place. *Never mind, I want Cassidy to be wrong. Wait . . . that would mean that Nolan would be right.* My head hurt.

Spared any more emotional anguish, I was jarred out of my thoughts by the sound of a phone being slammed on the ground. "Stupid phone!" Victor yelled.

Scrambling to my feet, I ran over to assess the damage. "What's wrong with you?!" I screamed. "That's our only phone, Victor!"

"A lot of good it's doing us. I can't even get a single bar!"

Picking up the cellular remains off a rock, I could tell that the patient was long gone. The glass screen was completely shattered. In a feeble attempt to keep hope alive, I pushed the power button several times. Nothing. Dangling the remains in front of Victor's face I angrily asked, "Happy now?"

"When we get back, I'll buy you a new one that isn't a piece of junk."

Not wanting to fight, I took a deep breath and bottled up the residual anger. "Okay," I said to the group, "it looks like the only way we're going to get home is to start walking."

"Wait a minute," Nolan objected, "we haven't even tried using the ball."

Cassidy was about to start yelling, but I managed to interject. "Do you know how to use it?"

"No," he admitted.

"Do you know what it does?"

"No."

"Are there any buttons, levers, or anything else on it that isn't solid metal?"

"No."

"Then I think we're walking."

"Well, I'm at least taking it with me!" he announced defiantly, scooping it up off the ground.

"Fine," I said, "who's stoppin' ya?"

"Ava…" Cassidy started to object.

I really liked Cassidy, but her high-strung anxiety was getting on my nerves. I was having enough trouble keeping my own emotions in check; I really didn't feel like dealing with hers. "Cassidy, enough!" She looked hurt by the rebuke, but I kept on, "I understand your concerns and I'm not saying that they aren't valid. But let's face it, we don't know where we are. Hopefully, we can find a road and get out of here ourselves. But if we can't, and Nolan wants to try to figure something out with that thing, then let him. It's not like we have a lot of options."

I'd felt confident saying those words, but seeing the look Cassidy gave me made me feel about two feet tall. "For all our sakes," she said, "you had better be right."

Twenty minutes into the journey and I already wanted to stop. The trees provided shade, but the heat still formed beads of sweat that streamed down my back, making my skin itch. *It's just my luck we get dumped in the woods on one of the hottest fall days of the year.* I took off my school jacket, tied it around my waist, and rolled up the sleeves of my blouse. The boys had been a step ahead of me, but instead of around their waists, they had tied their jackets around the metal ball to form a makeshift backpack. It was pretty clever, but I wasn't about to tell them that.

"I hate to be a buzz kill here, guys," Nolan said, "but what if we aren't headed toward the exit?" Everyone stopped walking and looked at him. "I mean, what if we're just heading deeper into the woods?"

"Well," I began, wracking my brain for an answer, "I mean . . ." Suddenly, I heard a noise. "What was that?!" Wide-eyed, I searched for the direction of the sound. The noise came again. It was a rattling of foliage and the snapping of twigs.

Victor rolled his eyes, "I'm sure it was noth . . ." but before he could finish, there was the distinct sound of a growl. "RUN!"

At Victor's command, we all took off into the woods. For the next several seconds, I didn't care where I was headed or who was with me. All I cared about was running as fast as I could. Trees whizzed past me, their branches reaching out and clawing at my arms. Boulders jutted up from the ground, threatening to send me face-first into the dirt. I could still hear the noises behind me. I may have been considered a fast runner, but I knew I was no match for an animal. Then, I saw what I needed. Right in front of me was a small pond.

It wasn't very big in size, but I was willing to bet that whatever was chasing me didn't want to go for a swim. Without hesitation, I leapt as far and as fast as I could into the center of the pond. My landing was part feet-first jump, part belly flop and I ended up fully submerged in the algae-covered water. Once I got my bearings, though, I found that the water was only shoulder height. Wiping the horrible-smelling liquid out of my eyes, I turned to see what had been trying to eat me. Standing on the edge of the pond, grunting angrily, was a pig! Okay, not exactly a pig. It was technically a wild boar. But I didn't care. I was now standing in the middle of a slime-covered cesspool thanks to a glorified piece of ham! After telling me off with a few angry grunts, it waddled off back into the forest.

I angrily slammed my fists on the water. "ARE YOU KIDDING ME?!" My voice reverberated through an empty forest, highlighting the fact that I was all alone. Where was everyone?

"CASSIDY? WINNIE?" I called out, trudging my way back onto dry land. "BOYS?" Nothing. "WHERE ARE YOU?!" Still nothing. The only sound was from birds moving through the trees. "Great . . ." I mumbled.

Picking out the comfiest looking rock, I took a seat. I felt the *squish* of my jacket. Untying it from around my waste, I threw it to the ground. It felt so good to get rid of it that I took off my tie and tossed that on the ground, too.

A cool breeze was exactly what I needed in that moment, but all I got was stale air. Instinctively, I reached for my phone to help pass the time, but then remembered its unfortunate demise. *They'd better find me fast*, I thought.

Thirty minutes went by, then an hour. My throat was sore and dry from the heat and frequent yelling for help. I looked over at the pond. *I am so not drinking that!* Standing up, I took one last look into the woods. I really didn't want to move on without them, but I wasn't sure what choice I had. For all I knew, they were miles away. No, I'd have to go it alone. Taking several calming breaths, I squared my shoulders and set off into the great unknown.

ERIN C.J. HANEY

9

CASSIDY

"NOLAN!" I screamed.

"WHAT?" he yelled back.

"I . . . THINK," I said gasping for air, "WE CAN STOP . . ." my lungs burned, "RUNNING!" Thankfully, he slowed down.

"Do you think it's gone?"

My response was a couple nods and a wheeze.

"Good, guess it knew not to mess with us!"

I just rolled my eyes.

"Where's everyone else?" he asked, looking around.

I tried to find them, but only saw trees. Mustering up what was left of my oxygen I yelled, "WINNIE? AVA?"

"DAVID, VICTOR . . . COME ON!" Nolan shouted with unexplainable confidence.

Nothing. Nada. Zilch. My stomach made a gurgling noise and I suddenly felt queasy. *Okay, don't panic,* I told myself. *It could be worse. You have Nolan. . . .* There was that queasy feeling again.

Nolan turned to me, "Where are they?"

My eyes bulged. "How would I know? I was following you!"

"Well, I don't know where they are. I was just running!"

Oh . . . my . . . goodness. Panic welled up in my chest as my eyes desperately searched the still woods. I was about to ask him if he wanted to go back, but when I turned, I saw that he was sitting on the ground, unwrapping the metal ball. "WHAT'S WRONG WITH YOU?!" I exclaimed, unable to comprehend what I was witnessing.

"What?" he asked innocently.

"Put that thing away!"

"No way!"

"I told you it's dangerous!"

"And I told *you* that it's our best chance of getting home."

"YOU. DON'T. KNOW. THAT!" I was at a loss for knowing how to get him to understand. I settled for using large arm movements and tiny jumps to wordlessly get my point across like some kind of interpretive dance. "You don't know what that thing does. You said it yourself. It could send us into outer space for all we know! Plus, even if it did take us home, our friends aren't with us!"

"Don't you think I know that? But I also know that finding them in these woods is about as likely as you being able to get a tan."

A ginger joke. Real original. As if I haven't heard 2 million of them!

"When it comes down to it, our best chance of getting our friends back is by getting out of here so we can send help!"

"I agree," I said suddenly.

"Uh . . . what?" The dumbfounded look on his face was almost worth having to agree with him.

"I agree. Our best chance is to get help. But not with *that*," I said, pointing at the ball. "Like I said, we don't know how it works. Even if we did get home, would we be able to get back?" He was silent. "Exactly! What we need to do is keep walking and try to get help around here. Once we find our friends then maybe . . . *maybe* . . . the ball can help us get home if we can't find another way."

With that, he stood up, slung the strap of the jacket-backpack over his shoulder, and said, "Deal!"

Our walk through the forest wasn't ideal, to put it lightly. The heat plus the lack of food and water made me dizzy and a bit nauseous. Even worse was the persistent feeling that something wasn't right about this place. But, no one can say that Cassidy McAdam can't make a boring walk entertaining!

Surprisingly, Nolan wasn't much of a talker, but I wasn't going to let that stop me. "Seriously, I didn't do anything to the ball," I explained. "It just started spinning! I dropped it because, like, how else do you respond to a spinning metal thing? Then there was a blue light. Did you see it?"

"Yeah, I saw it," he confirmed.

"I wonder why it was blue. Why blue? Why not white or yellow or red? Strange . . . anyway, I saw it grow bigger and bigger. At first, I thought I was seeing things. But then, the next thing I know, I'm like, falling!"

"Yeah, I was there."

"The train! Did you hear the train sound?"

"Yeah."

"It was just like the sound that Tessa said her mom said that students from the 70's said they heard when Dr. Keller was working on his experiments. People thought I was crazy to believe the stories, but they won't think I'm crazy now! I just know Dr. Keller is behind this. Don't you think?"

"Uh-huh."

This went on for about an hour. He didn't seem to know much more than I did, so I switched topics. "Are you hungry? I'm hungry. I want to eat so bad! Man, I'd love a pint of ice cream right about now. Chocolate and peanut butter—no—cotton candy. Could you mix cotton candy and chocolate together? Why haven't they done that? Can't they put chocolate on anything? Like a bug. I've heard about them putting chocolate on bugs. Would you eat a chocolate-covered bug?"

This topic lasted about an hour and a half before Nolan spoke up, "Cassidy, to answer your first question—which I can't believe I remember—yes, I am hungry. So hungry, in fact, that I would really appreciate it if you would please stop talking about food."

"Sorry." The newfound sound of silence felt awkward. What could I talk about? It wasn't as if Nolan and I had much in common and he certainly wasn't helping carry the conversation. Then I got an idea, "Hey Nolan, let's play some travel games! I'll get it started. I spy something beginning with 'T.'"

There was a pause. He let out a heavy sigh before slowly saying, "Tree."

"You got it! Good job! Now it's your turn." Several more rounds of "I Spy," a few games of "20 Questions," and one solo performance of the song "99 Bottles of Root Beer" later, and we were back to playing "I Spy" again.

Nolan was moving slower than usual as he droned, "I spy something beginning with 'T.'"

Seriously? Is he even trying? "Is it trees?" I asked.

"Yeah."

"Nolan, I already said that one!"

Nolan stopped and whipped around to face me. "WHAT ELSE IS THERE, CASSIDY?" His sudden outburst was shocking. "Look around you! We're in the middle OF THE WOODS!"

I heard the rattling of trees coming from the direction we'd been heading.

"Worst of all, I'm in the middle of the woods with YOU!"

His comment stung, but I let him continue. My attention was transfixed on the continuous movement I was hearing. Clearly, Nolan wasn't aware of it as he proceeded to take his frustrations out on me.

"I mean, of all the people in the world I could have been stranded with, I had to be stranded with the one person on the planet who never gets sick of the sound of her own voice!"

"Uh, Nolan . . ." I squeaked out, my eyes transfixed on what was now before me.

"Did you not pick up on the fact that I wasn't really responding? Was that not even a *clue*?"

I couldn't move. Fear had cemented my feet to the ground. "Nolan . . ."

He didn't stop. If anything, he got even more impassioned, allowing his hands to gesture wildly about. "Tell me Cassidy, you're the president of the Public Speaking Club, do the other members even get to *talk*? I've heard people say that redheads have no soul, but does that mean they have no *filter*?"

"Who has no soul?" came the deep voice of a stranger.

Nolan froze. Slowly turning around, he found himself face-to-muzzle with a large, grey horse. Trailing his eyes upward, he caught sight of its rider. The man was tall with thick muscles. He wore a long-sleeve dark-brown shirt and pants. His vest, shoes, and belt were made of thick leather

60

and on his right hip, the sun's gleam signaled the presence of a dagger. Even more threatening, was the leather strap running across his chest that held a sword so long it was probably more than half my height.

What Nolan seemed to notice most, however, was what surrounded the man's large eyes and thick jaw—long hair and a beard as red as fire!

"Did I say redheads?" Nolan stammered. "I didn't mean redheads. I mean, I didn't mean *you* . . . . It's a joke! You know, just something stupid that people say." The man's gaze never faltered, which only made Nolan struggle harder to dig himself out of the verbal hole he'd created. "I love redheads. All of them! Little Orphan Annie . . . Archie . . . Clifford the Big Red . . ." His voice wavered before suddenly shouting, "WHAT'S THAT?" Pointing at nothing, he ran.

For a few brief moments, I envied him, wishing I had run. That is, of course, until he fell into a hole. One minute, he was sprinting wildly through a clearing in the trees. The next, he was sprawled out on the ground with his right leg buried in the earth up to his knee. Instinctively, I ran to him.

Before I could get there, the man had guided his horse over to Nolan and dismounted. Extending his hand, he said, "You should mind where you're running." I noticed he had a rolling Scottish accent, which made his baritone voice quite charming.

Nolan looked at the hand with uncertainty. Finally deciding to accept it, he was lifted up onto level ground.

"I suppose I should thank you," the man said.

"Why?" Nolan asked.

"Because," a smile spread across his face, "I now know the pits work."

"*You* made that hole?"

"Aye, my men did. We dug all the pits along this here clearing." He gestured his hand toward an opening in the trees.

"What pits?" Nolan asked, struggling to see them.

The man let out a hearty laugh and hit him on the shoulder, seemingly unaware of his own strength. "Why, they're camouflaged my boy! Hidden from view with brushwood and grass. What good would it do me to have a bunch of holes that the enemy could *see*?"

I suddenly got that nervous feeling in the pit of my stomach again. "Enemy?" I asked, finding my voice for the first time.

He looked at me with a strange curiosity. "Well, the English of course!"

I didn't like what I was hearing. The accent . . . the outfit . . . talking about "the English." Either this man was a completely crazy, hole-digging man living in the woods, or else . . . I really didn't want to consider the other possibility.

Narrowing his eyes, he seemed to take notice of our attire for the first time. "You two aren't from around these parts are you?"

"Why do you say that?" I asked.

"Well, aside from your strange manner of dress and the way you speak, from the look in your eyes, I get the feeling that you don't know who I am."

"Should we?" Nolan nervously asked.

Again, the man let out a hearty laugh. "Why, I find that most people are able to recognize their king."

"You're a king?"

"King Robert Bruce, at your service." The man gave a chivalrous bow.

Again, I felt my stomach churn. My heart started racing. Although the man seemed nice enough so far, I didn't like what I was hearing. I found myself internally pleading, *Please be a lunatic, please be a lunatic.* Unfortunately, though, he didn't give off "crazy" vibes. I didn't want to ask, but I had to make sure. "Uh, Robert . . ." I began, "King Robert . . . this may sound like a strange question, but what year is it?"

He and Nolan both looked at me as if trying to determine my level of sanity. Then King Robert smiled politely and said, "It would be the year of our Lord 1314."

Nolan and I looked at each other in horror. Blood draining from my face, I felt no joy as I choked out, "I told you so."

10

AVA

To the tune of *This is the Song That Never Ends* I sang:

"This is the walk that never ends,"

It came out in a monotone voice that made the song sound more like a funeral dirge than the classic car-ride sing-along that inspired my slightly altered lyrics. Still, I continued:

"Yes, it goes on and on my friends.
Some people fell through a big blue hole
not knowing what it was,
now they'll continue walking around forever
just because
this is the walk that never . . ."

The next line stuck in my throat and I wondered if I was hallucinating. A road. There was a road! Small and unpaved, sure, but it was the most beautiful road I'd ever laid my eyes on. Newfound energy surged through my veins as I ran toward it. I was about to be saved! Looking around, I didn't see any buildings or signs of life. Oh well. If there was a road, there had to be people or a building somewhere.

I walked along the path for quite a while before finally sitting down. With every bend in the road I thought, *Something will be right around the corner. I can't be far from help.* Yet, there hadn't been anything around any of the corners and, clearly, help was very far away. What made me finally stop was my overwhelming hunger, thirst, and a sharp pain coming from my feet.

Taking off my socks and shoes I saw for the first time the damage I'd done to them. As it turns out, walking around in wet socks isn't a good idea. The water had made my skin wrinkled and weak. To make matters worse, I hadn't broken in my new school shoes, which caused painful blisters. What was I going to do if it hurt to walk?

Don't lose hope, I told myself. *You don't have to walk. Someone is bound to drive by. It's only a matter of time.*

"This is the road that no one drives,"

Keeping the tune of my previous song, I made a few lyrical revisions:

"There is no way I will survive,"

Slumped up against a hill, I'd been waiting for rescue for over an hour. The longer I waited, the angrier I got. And the angrier I got, the louder I sang:

"One MORON started sitting here
not giving up on hope,
and she'll continue sitting here
forever like a dope . . ."

"EVERYBODY NOW!" I yelled out. After pausing a moment, waiting for a group of invisible people to join me in song, I buried my face in my hands and mumbled, "I'm officially losing my mind."

"*Pssst,*" I thought I heard.

Startled, I whipped my head back and forth looking for the source of the noise. I didn't see anything. *Uh-oh. I really am losing my mind.*

"*Pssst,*" the sound came again. This time, I distinctly heard it coming from behind me. Turning around, I saw someone up on the hill hiding behind a rock.

Jumping to my feet, I grabbed a stone and prepared to take aim. Even though I'd been waiting to get help from someone, I wasn't about to trust a stranger lurking in the woods. "STAY WHERE YOU ARE," I shouted. "I'm trained in Krav Maga and I'm not afraid to use it!" I knew I didn't look intimidating, but I wasn't lying about my training in the Israeli martial art. If he stepped any closer, he was going to find out just how truthful I was.

Popping his head higher above the rock, I got a better look at him. He was young-ish, maybe in his 20's? I couldn't be sure. It was hard to get a good look at his face through the shoulder-length jet-black hair that fell in front of it. His pale skin and thin frame gave him a look reminiscent of a vampire. I gripped my rock tighter.

"If I were you, I'd keep my voice down," he whispered. He had an accent. Irish? Scottish? I didn't know, but I did pick up on a slight lisp as he said the word "voice."

"Oh, you want me to be quiet? HELP! HELP!" I yelled at the top of my lungs.

Panic stricken, he jumped up and took a couple of steps toward me. I threw the rock, missing his head by less than an inch. Quickly I picked up another. Steely determination in my eyes, I readied myself for a fight. "I've got plenty more where that came from and I promise you I won't miss again."

A flash of anger could be seen in his dark eyes, but it quickly cooled into panic when he heard a faint rumbling sound. His gaze darted to his left, then back at me. "If I were you," he said, "I'd heed my advice and get off the road. . . . Or there's no tellin' what'll come of ya." With that, he scrambled up the hillside and disappeared behind the trees.

His words made me nervous, but what really scared me was the look in his eyes. When I looked behind the intensity, I saw sincerity. *Yeah right,* I told myself, pushing down my anxiety. *As if I'm gonna listen to some freak in the woods!*

I stood there for a few moments, listening to the rumbling coming down the road. The sound grew louder and louder. "Good," I said, "now I can finally get rescued." Dropping the rock, I picked up my shoes and socks that I'd left drying in the sun. Not willing to put the tiny torture devices back on my feet, I tucked the bundle up under my arm and waited. *What kind of a car is that?* It sounded big and heavy and metallic, as if all its parts had a few loose bolts that were making them rattle. It was also moving slower than I expected. *Watch this thing break down right when it gets to me!*

As it came closer, though, I realized that it wasn't a car at all. Squinting, I made out the image of horses—A LOT of horses. Losing my nerve, I darted into the woods and ducked behind a tree. "What's happening?" I breathed, struggling to bring down my increasing heart rate.

A few moments later, the sound was right behind me. Pressing my back against the tree, I closed my eyes and prayed to be invisible. *Ava, you coward,* I chastised myself, *what if that's your rescue and you're missing it because you're cowering behind a tree? But what if it isn't? What if Vampire Dude was telling the truth?* The only thing I knew for sure was that this wasn't normal. And I really missed normal. I made a vow right then and there that if I ever got back to normal that I would cherish it, savor it.

I expected the noise to be long gone after a few minutes, but it wasn't. It kept going and going. There was only one way to find out what I was dealing with, and that was to look. Slowly turning around, I cautiously peered around the tree. I couldn't believe what I was looking at. Yes, there were horses, but they weren't just any horses. These horses where covered in flowing fabrics of all different colors. Their riders were dressed like medieval knights, wearing head-to-toe metal armor with swords strapped around their waists. The sun reflecting off the polished silver was almost blinding. Covering their chest, each rider wore a cloth garment that matched the colors and patterns of their horse. There were also men on foot, some wearing more armor than others, yet all marching in unison.

"It's an army," I said aloud, though quiet enough for my words to be drowned out by the ruckus of the caravan. Mind racing to rationalize what I was seeing, I thought, *Maybe this is some kind of publicity stunt or a group of actors filming a movie.* I searched for any signs that would prove my theory. I didn't see any cameras or crew members dressed in t-shirts. Surely if the foot soldiers were background extras, at least some of them would be overacting. I searched their faces, but every gesture and facial expression looked authentic. Sweat and dirt clung to them and the vacant look of fatigue covered their eyes.

After what seemed like an eternity, the parade of knights ended and so began a multitude of people dressed in simple clothing, riding with carts packed full of goods. *Where's the end of this thing?* I was getting impatient. A fly was bugging me, but I didn't dare swat it and risk being seen. Instead, I was forced to endure the abuse.

Suddenly, I didn't care about the fly anymore. I didn't care about anything around me. My vision became laser-focused on a flash of green plaid and navy. To my horror, I saw Winnie. She was riding in the back of a wooden cart and her hands were tied. She looked like she was crying, and it took everything in my power not to go chasing after her. But even with my Krav Maga, there was nothing I could do against an army that big and that powerful. I was forced to watch her be wheeled away.

Then I saw David and Victor. Their hands and feet were also tied, but they weren't being given as smooth of a ride. They had both been flopped over a horse like two sacks of potatoes. Even after my friends had long faded from view, I kept staring into the distance, watching as clouds of dust slowly fell back to earth. The rattling noise gradually faded away, until there was nothing left.

Turning my back against the tree, I slid down it until I hit the rocky ground. My hands shook. My breathing became labored. Gasping for air, the piercing sting of emerging tears assaulted my eyes. I had to pull myself together. *You can't do this right now. You have to be stronger than this. You are stronger than this!* I focused on my breathing. Inhale. Exhale.

Slowly, I pulled myself onto my feet. I wasn't going to panic. I was going to take control. I knew what I was going to do. I was going to find that vampire!

ERIN C.J. HANEY

11

DAVID

"Just wait 'til my father hears about this!" Victor threatened. "He's gonna sue that school for everything they've got!"

"You just couldn't stop talking," I mumbled.

"Hey, this isn't my fault!"

I couldn't believe what I was hearing. It was entirely his fault!

"OW!" I yelled as our horse hopped over a rock, putting pressure on my stomach and flopping my face into its side. Spitting and sputtering I yelled at Victor, "I shouldn't know what horse hair tastes like!"

"Stop your whining," was his callous reply. "At least you got the front of the horse."

Sometimes, there was justice in the world.

Truly, though, I had no idea how Victor could claim that our capture wasn't his fault. My mind wandered back to the moment right before we'd seen the soldiers:

After walking in the woods for hours, we were literally dancing for joy (some of us better than others) as soon as we found a road. We became even more excited when we heard something coming our way. However, it wasn't a normal sound. Winnie said it sounded like horses and carts. She had been right, of course, but Victor wasn't worried.

"So what if it is?" he asked. "It's probably the Amish. As long as the buggy's headed toward the exit, you won't hear me complaining."

But the sound got louder and louder. "That sounds like a lot of Amish," I said, my voice shaking.

Victor dismissively replied, "Maybe they're having a convention. Like, BuggyCon or somethin'."

In hindsight, we should have run right then and there. But I suppose, in our desperation to be rescued, it felt like our only option was to wait for whatever was coming. Either that, or else we were just plain stupid.

Standing near a bend in the road, we stared intensely at the rocky outcropping that was blocking our view of what was to come. Finally, we saw it: a medieval procession like nothing anyone could have imagined. Majestic horses stomping their hooves into the ground, stirring up clouds of dust; knights reflecting the sun's brilliance with their chainmail and armor; and an array of colored flags, held high on poles, waving in the breeze. The most impressive, of which, had been a large red flag held high above the rest. Three elongated lions were stacked on top of one another, their claws ready to attack. And attack they did.

The procession stopped the moment they saw us and a young knight dressed in yellow and red rode our direction. "Who goes there and what is the reasoning for blocking the way of His Majesty?"

I was frozen—a mixture of shock and fear. "Go on, what say you?" he demanded, his English accent helping him sound only slightly more polite.

Unfortunately, Victor's mouth wasn't as frozen as mine. "I get what's going on," Victor said, laughing as he wagged his finger at the knight. "You guys really had me going there for a minute. The horses, the armor . . . man, you guys must have sunk a lot of money into those costumes!"

Wide-eyed, I whipped my head towards him. Was he out of his mind? We were being interrogated by a guy who dressed himself like the human equivalent of a Transformer and he had *laughed*.

70

The knight remained stone-faced. Internally I begged, *Please, Victor, stop talking!* But he didn't stop. In fact, he continued his monologue in what was an incredibly poor representation of a British accent.

"Well done, chap! Pip pip, cheerio, and God save the Queen! You'll be quite the smash at the renaissance festival, but right now it would be brilliant if you could give us a lift as I could really use a loo."

At that moment, I knew we were doomed. Clearly, unlike myself, Victor had never been to a renaissance festival. If he had, he would have known that people don't ride into them by the THOUSANDS!

The knight growled, "Your words sound like the words of a rebel. Do you stand with Bruce?"

Victor turned to me and mumbled out of the corner of his mouth, "Geez, this guy refuses to drop the act." Turning back to him, he belted out, "Yes, we stand with Bruce! Long live King Bruce! May he rule over the entire kingdom . . . blah, blah, blah. Now are you gonna take us with you or what?"

Yes, it had been entirely his fault.

"How was I supposed to know they weren't in costume?" Victor asked defensively. It really didn't matter what he'd done, there was no way he was going to accept the blame. It occurred to me, in that moment, that in the five years we'd been friends, I had never once heard him say he was sorry. "Where I come from, people aren't arrested for jaywalking by guys with swords," he continued. "Geez, I knew that ball wasn't normal but— dude—I didn't expect this. The gross negligence of Providence for allowing this to happen is ridiculous. My father will make them pay. He'll make them all pay!"

I'd never met Victor's father, but since he was only ever mentioned when Victor wanted to scare someone, I couldn't help picturing him as Marlon Brando in *The Godfather*. Albeit, I'd never actually seen the movie, but that iconic image of a mobster who wanted to make people "sleep with the fishes" was enough to make me glad Victor's dad wasn't big on school visits.

"Well, if I were you, I'd stop talking about what your dad's gonna do and start thinking about what we're gonna do. We have to find a way to get out of here before . . . it doesn't matter. We just need to get out of here." I refused to think any further. I wasn't prepared to contemplate the possible outcomes of this situation. Not yet.

Victor, on the other hand, didn't seem too bothered. "Don't worry about it," he said. "When we have a chance to stop and talk to them, I'll sort this out in a matter of minutes."

"Don't you think your mouth has done enough damage?"

"Again, not my fault. But now that I know what kind of people we're dealing with, I'm ready to speak their language."

"Please don't do that accent again."

"I'm talking about a bribe, David! I've seen my dad do it a thousand times. Give people some money, and they let you off the hook."

Like I said, his dad sounded like a scary mob boss. "I don't care what your father does, bribery is wrong, Victor!"

"Oh, and you have a better idea?"

I wracked my brain, thinking through different scenarios. Three kids . . . thousands of armed soldiers . . . none of the possibilities had a happy ending. Reluctantly, I asked, "Do you have anything to bribe them with?"

"Of course I do! Check my shoe." Bending his knees, he raised his feet up in the air. It took some effort, but I was able to grab the thin wallet he'd stuffed in his sock.

I made the mistake of breathing. "Ewww Victor! This wallet smells like your feet!"

"Hey, it's not my fault it's a hot day!"

Of course it wasn't. Coughing, I opened up the wallet and took out the contents. "THESE ARE CREDIT CARDS!"

"With a $20,000 limit *each.* You're welcome!"

"Take a look around you! Does it look like they take Discover here?"

"You don't know for sure. Technically, we still don't know where we are. We could be in a different part of the world where people think it's cool to dress up like soldiers, yet still enjoy modern conveniences."

I doubted even he believed that, but I figured I'd put the theory to rest. "Let's find out," I declared. Looking around, I saw a young boy, about my age, walking near our horse. I tried to get his attention, "Excuse me . . . um . . . hello . . ."

"HEY, DUDE," Victor shouted at him, "we've got a question."

He looked at us with disdain. "I am not a 'dude.' I am a squire serving the honorable Gilbert de Clare, 8th Earl of Gloucester. And I'm not to engage with prisoners."

I had no idea what any of that meant and I didn't really care. I just needed this dude, sorry, *squire* to talk. "Hey, I understand, it's hard to trust a couple of guys tied up on a horse. I just have a couple of questions and then I'll leave you alone, promise. First question: Where are we?"

He looked straight ahead, pretending like he hadn't heard me.

"Okay, let's try something easier. *When* are we?"

He didn't answer. I had to change tactics, and fast, or else I'd lose him. "Okay, don't talk to me. Just nod your head for 'yes' and shake your head for 'no.'" Holding up one of Victor's credit cards, I asked, "Do you know what this is?"

Looking at it out of the corner of his eye, I could see he was curious. He turned to grab for it, but I quickly pulled it away. "Eh, eh, eh . . . where are we?"

He looked visibly conflicted on whether or not to answer the question. Luckily for me, his curiosity got the better of him, "Scotland, on our way to Stirling." He grabbed for it, but I pulled it back again.

"What is the date today?"

"The 22nd of June in the year of our Lord 1314. The day before His Highness King Edward II, ruler of England and Wales, demolishes the Scottish forces and puts an end to Robert Bruce once and for all."

I was stunned. I'd obsessively watched enough time traveling movies to suspect that that's what had happened, but what really shocked me was the name he'd said. I'd actually heard it before! "R . . . R . . . Robert Bruce," I stammered, "Robert *the* Bruce?"

"Yes," he said matter-of-factly, snatching the credit card out of my hand. "Though it would be more accurate to refer to him as Robert the Outlaw." He ran his fingers over the credit card and bent it back and forth a few times. I'd never seen someone so enamored with a piece of plastic! Lost in his own world, his pace slowed, causing us to ride past him. Whatever, it didn't matter. I had gotten the information I wanted.

"Congratulations," Victor said sarcastically, "You just paid him $10,000 a question."

"No, I gave him a worthless piece of plastic. Weren't you listening? We're in 1314! So, unless you've got something more valuable, like gold or silver . . ."

"Sorry, I don't wear jewelry. But they seem to like plastic . . ."

"Yeah, because all it took to get it was answering a couple of questions. It'll take a lot more than that to convince them to let us go. Face it, the bribery plan is off the table."

Changing topics, Victor asked, "So, how have you heard of this Robert guy?"

"You mean besides when you told them that you wanted him to rule over all the land?"

"It wasn't my . . ."

"Yeah, yeah, it wasn't your fault. Got it. Anyway, I don't really know him. I just remember my brother talking about him after he'd watched some movie."

"Really? What did he tell you?"

"Honestly, I don't remember much. It was a long time ago, but I do remember him saying that Robert was a powerful warrior and that he had a claim to the Scottish throne. I thought, though, that he'd said he was on the side of the English."

Victor scoffed, "Well, clearly that isn't true."

"Yeah, well, have you ever tried doing a history report based on a movie?"

"No."

"Well, trust me, it's a bad idea! It's amazing how many writers don't even try for historical accuracy."

"Yeah, yeah, it's a real shame," Victor said. I may not have seen the eye roll, but I felt it. "What I'm hearing is that all we know about this guy is what your brother told you was in a movie that we can't trust. Oh, and that he's an outlaw."

"Basically . . . yes. But technically, they seem to consider us outlaws, so I'd say the bar is set pretty low."

"Which means we know even less. Great," he mumbled.

Our horse slowed and then came to a halt. People in the caravan began moving about, unpacking supplies.

"What's going on?" Victor asked.

"I don't know," I said. "I guess we've reached our destination."

74

A knight covered in gold fleur-de-lis approached us. He had salt and pepper hair, pointy ears, and sharp features. If I was casting a movie villain, I'd give him the part.

I was surprised to hear a French accent as he said, "We are resting for the night." He then grabbed the back of Victor's shirt collar.

Anticipating the worst, I tried to stall. "WAIT, WAIT, WAIT! Who are you?"

His smile was menacing. "I'm sorry, allow me to introduce myself. I am Sir Henry de Beaumont, 4th Earl of Buchan. Welcome to Falkirk." Immediately, he pulled on Victor's collar, sending him falling to the ground in a giant heap. So much for a friendly welcome.

"Ow . . ." Victor moaned.

Sir Henry looked at me and his twisted smile grew. *Uh-oh.*

"Hey, why don't you tell me a little about Falkirk," I blurted out at lightning speed, doing everything I could to postpone the inevitable. "What's the population here? Are there any good places to eat? Does Travelocity rate it five stars? . . . OWWW!" The pain came swift and fierce. Lying in the dirt, I looked up and saw Sir Henry staring down at me. "So far . . ." I winced, "I'd give it one star."

12

AVA

I wasn't sure what was worse: running in ill-fitting shoes, or running barefoot through the forest. It was a toss-up. But since putting on shoes would require more time, I opted to endure the sharp jabs from rocks and twigs.

"HEY!" I screamed. "WHERE ARE YOU?" I wasn't sure if I would ever be able to find the stranger in the woods, but I had to try. He seemed to know what was going on, and I needed answers.

Struggling up a rocky side of the hill, I was relieved to see the landscape start to even out and the trees begin to thin. Running toward the top of the hill, I saw the dark-haired stranger standing with a small group of men. Finally, my luck was beginning to change!

"HEY YOU!" I yelled, running toward them.

An older guy, with a grey beard, pulled his dagger. The dark-haired stranger grabbed the guy's arm, signaling to him that I wasn't a threat. The older gentleman sheathed his dagger, but it was a reminder to me that I should approach with caution. "Look, I don't want any trouble," I said when I reached them, "but I have some questions."

"You know this lass?" the older guy asked.

The dark-haired stranger answered, "I found her lying by the road, warned her to hide herself before the English arrived." He turned to me and added, "I'm glad to see you heeded my advice."

"Um, yeah, thanks," I said nervously. "Here's the thing. I'm not from around here."

The dark-haired stranger looked at my outfit and chuckled, "I didn't think ya were. The way you dress is quite unusual. In what land do people wear such clothes?"

"Providence," I replied bitterly.

"Providence? I've never heard of such a place."

"Be grateful. Anyway, can you tell me where we are?"

"Scotland, land of the mighty King Robert Bruce!" The men let out a loud cheer.

"Wow," I said, not sure of how to respond to such enthusiasm, "okay . . . um . . . what's today's date?"

"The 22nd of June."

"And the year?"

"1314 of course."

I felt dizzy. *Keep it together, Ava,* I told myself. *Focus on one thing at a time. You won't be able to save your friends by panicking.* To the dark-haired stranger I asked, "Here's another question: Who are you?"

With a mischievous smile and a dramatic bow, he announced, "I am . . . The Black Douglas."

There was an awkward pause as the men waited to see how I would respond. "Uh . . . okay," I said. "Nice to meet you."

The older guy looked bewildered. "Do they not tell stories or sing lullabies where you come from?"

"They do . . ." I said slowly, "but I'm sorry, I don't know who you are." I was afraid I'd offended him, but to my surprise, The Black Douglas didn't seem bothered.

"Just as well," he said, "best you not be scared of me."

That didn't sound good. "Should I be?" I asked, taking a step back.

He laughed, "Only if you believe everything you hear, and I wouldn't advise that."

I felt slightly better until the older guy added, "That's right, only some of the stories are true."

"Don't scare the wee lass," The Black Douglas said after taking a look at my face. "She quite enjoys throwing rocks." He added a wink and I couldn't help but smile. It was strange. One minute he was frightening, and the next minute he was completely charming. I was having trouble making up my mind about him.

"Well, in case it matters to ya," the older guy said, "I'm Keith, Robert Keith."

Instinctively I wanted to say, "Bond, James Bond." Instead, I kept it simple with, "Nice to meet you."

"So," Keith said, crossing his burly arms across his chest, "what is it that a young lass, such as yourself, be doing out in these here woods?"

"Uh . . ." I hesitated, not wanting to say something that would get me into trouble later, "I'm looking for my friends."

"I see," he said. "Would they be the ones we saw ridin' with the English?"

I was stunned. How did he know? The Black Douglas must have read my expression, because he hurriedly explained, "We were closely observing the English army and saw three youth dressed in your unusual attire. It doesn't take a clever man to figure it out."

"Oh, I see. Then you know that they were captured."

"Aye," he said.

"Can you help me get them back?"

He shared an uneasy look with Keith. "That, I'm sorry to say, we cannot do."

"Why not?" I was getting frustrated. "You know more about them than I do. You clearly don't like them, and you've got weapons. Isn't there something you can do? I mean, you said it yourself; you're The Black Douglas, someone to be feared, someone people tell stories about. You're telling me you can't do anything?"

Completely unfazed by my frustration, he calmly replied, "You're right, I do know more about them than you do. I know enough to know that it would be a fool's errand for me and my men to try to free a group of prisoners now—especially as we prepare to fight them in battle."

"You're going to fight them?" I asked, surprised by that additional piece of information.

"Aye, we came to these woods to get a good look at the men we will soon be facing on the battlefield. I am sorry about your friends, truly I am, but right now my loyalty is to my country. King Edward II, ruler of England and Wales, is following in his father's footsteps by trying to take the country from its rightful ruler, King Robert the Bruce. If he succeeds in this upcoming battle and takes control of Stirling Castle, he will be one step closer to completing his mission," a grim look came over his face as he added, "and the Scottish army may not be able to recover."

What can a person possibly say after something like that? It's not as if I could tell them, "Sorry to hear about your country and all the people in it, but I'd really love for you to forget about that and help save my friends." No, I couldn't say that. I had to face facts. The only person I could count on right now to save my friends, was me. I was enveloped in a wave of despair. *How am I supposed to do this? I'm just one person. I can't even get a "B" on my math homework, let alone save my friends from an army!*

"There may be one thing I can do," he said suddenly. Eagerly, I looked up at him. "I can take you back to our camp at Stirling. There, you will have food and rest." It may have seemed like a small gesture, but considering how hungry and exhausted I was, his offer was music to my ears!

"That would be great. Thank you!"

He turned to get the horses, but abruptly stopped and looked back at me. With a smile he said, "And it's James, by the way."

"What?" I asked, momentarily confused.

"My name . . . is James Douglas."

Our ride through the forest was exhilarating! The men wanted to get to Stirling quickly so that they could tell King Robert details about what the English army looked like. Consequently, they rode like the wind! Darting through forests, streaking across grassland, I watched as the sky turned vibrant orange, encircled by swirls of pink. My problems were left behind, at least for a little while, as I took a deep breath of fresh air. This land was absolutely beautiful!

"It won't be much farther now," James said, "that's Stirling Castle over there." In the distance, I could see a stout, brick structure hoisted into the air by steep, jagged cliffs which were surrounded by a halo of cloud-like trees. Both beautiful and imposing, my eyes were drawn to it like a magnet.

"I think Scotland's gonna win, James," I said encouragingly. "I can't see how the English could possibly break through that castle!"

"They don't have to," he growled. "They're in control of it."

"WHAT?" I couldn't believe what I was hearing. "I thought that was the whole point, to stop them from taking the castle."

"It is."

"But they have the castle."

"They do."

I was so confused. Luckily, he explained, "Our war with England has lasted for many years, and throughout those years, the English have controlled many a castle in Scotland, including Stirling. It's made them strong. For a while now, we've been laying siege to such castles, taking back control over what's rightfully ours. We've been smart about it, too, often surrounding the castles and cutting them off from needed supplies like food and drink. Then they surrender to us without a fight."

"That sounds like a good strategy. Why don't you just do that with Stirling Castle?"

"That was our plan. We'd surrounded them and were camped out for over three months waiting for their surrender. Then King Robert's brother, Edward—the impatient goat—decided he would strike a deal with them instead."

"What kind of a deal?"

"That if King Edward II did not send an army to rescue the castle within a year's time, the English would surrender the castle to Scotland. Otherwise, the castle would remain under English control."

"But Kind Edward is sending an army. We just saw it. So…when's the deadline?"

"The 24th of June."

"That's in two days!" I wasn't sure why we were even having this conversation if King Edward was clearly going to make it on time. I felt bad for the Scottish people, but what's done was done. "Isn't this battle already over?"

"Hah!" he sneered. "Spoken like someone who doesn't know King Edward!"

In all fairness, I didn't. "What do you mean?" I asked.

"King Robert isn't just another rival king. The English see him as a traitor, an outlaw, and the fact that he's even still *breathing* is considered a great humiliation to England. King Edward has just marched an army of his best men all the way from England to Scotland, to where King Robert the Bruce is now waiting. Some may think he will honor the agreement and allow us to go in peace, but I say it's foolish to believe such things. There is too much hatred that flows through his veins. No, even King Robert knows that we must prepare for battle."

Despite the warm summer breeze, I felt a chill creep up my spine.

"We've arrived," he said, slowing the horse down and bringing him to a stop. Though it was getting late, the campsite was still buzzing with activity. Tents had been pitched, fires were blazing, and deep, reverberating laughter could be heard from soldiers who were done working for the day.

"I'll be back," James said, sliding off the horse. "Stay here. I have to talk with the king. Then I'll take you to the valley where the camp followers have hidden themselves." *Camp followers?*

I watched as he and Keith disappeared into a large tent internally illuminated by the warm glow of several candles.

"What do ya think?" I heard someone say. Searching for the source of the voice, I saw it was coming from a young man standing by one of the campfires. He held his arms out, showcasing a thick-quilted brown jacket. "Beatrice finished fixing the stitching on my aketon. Do I look ready for battle?"

"I think any stitching would look good to you if it came from Beatrice," joked a burly guy as he lazily poked at the fire with a stick.

The young man looked offended. "That's not true! I simply have an appreciation for her work."

The burly guy didn't look like he was buying it. He got up and studied the jacket. "I don't know. You need a helmet." He picked up a metal hat with a wide brim and placed it on his head. "And, of course, you need a spear." He handed the young man a wooden spear taller than himself. Taking a moment to study the resulting ensemble, he clicked his tongue and said, "Well, I say, you do look like a soldier. . . . And maybe when you finally grow up little boy, you'll get to be a real one!" As the group of men around the campfire laughed, the young man took off his helmet and playfully swatted the burly man with it before joining the rest of them in laughter and jokes.

Under normal circumstances, it would have been a sweet scene. A bunch of guys joking with each other and having fun. But these were not normal circumstances. It occurred to me that before long, they would be out fighting on a battlefield. The worst part was that if what the young man was wearing was, indeed, what they planned to fight in, they were in a whole lot of trouble! The English were covered in armor, not puffy quilts and metal hats. They also had swords instead of big, pointy sticks. And where were the horses? The English had horses as far as the eye could see! I looked around in a desperate attempt to spot therm. I saw a few hundred, but that was it. It was nothing by comparison!

The laughter around the campfire became a dark, hollow sound as I looked at the face of the young man who had a crush on a girl named Beatrice and thought, *They're going to lose.*

ERIN C.J. HANEY

13

AVA

We rode over the northern hillside in silence. Before we'd left, James Douglas had told me that, by the king's orders, I was not to breathe a word of what I'd seen of the English army. Apparently, the king felt it would hurt the soldiers' morale.

Ya think? I internally screamed. *I'm not going into battle and even I want to stay as far away from them as humanly possible!* It had been the stern look in James' eyes that clamped my mouth shut. All I could muster was a simple nod of understanding.

That look. That soul-piercing look. I was starting to understand why he'd been given the nickname "The Black Douglas."

Descending into a valley, we reached the camp. A mixture of tents and crude wooden structures were set up like a little village. Smoke billowed up from the campfires as both men and women scurried around pulling carts, carrying baskets, hammering down tent pegs. As we got closer, the scent of the smoke reached my nose, carrying with it the smell of roasted meat. My stomach growled. *Food!*

"We've arrived," said James as he slid off the horse, then extended his arm to help me down. "Come, sit down over here by the fire and I'll see to it that you get some food and shelter. You'll be safe here." Then he left.

I stared into the flames, my mind foggy and dizzy. *What do I do now? I'm all alone. I'm starving. I'm stuck in the past. Winnie, David, and Victor are being held captive. As for Cassidy and Nolan, who knows? They could be anywhere.*

"Is that . . .?" came a distant voice. *That voice sounds like Cassidy,* I thought, my eyes welling up with tears. *How many times at Providence had I wanted her to stop talking? Now, what I wouldn't give to hear her voice again!*

"IT IS!" The voice sounded closer and more real this time. *It can't be . . .*

BAM! A big bear hug from behind took me by surprise as I toppled off the log I had been sitting on. "What in the . . ." before I could finish the sentence, someone grabbed my shoulders and whipped me around. It *was* Cassidy!

"I can't believe it's really you," she squealed. "I was praying and praying that we'd find you and the others and here you are! It's a miracle! How did you find this place? Do you know where we are? Do you know *when* we are? If you don't then you're in for a shock and you might want to sit down. Oh wait, you already are sitting down. . . ."

"CASSIDY! I'm glad to see you, too." Yep, it was really Cassidy.

"Sorry, I'm just so excited! Nolan and I were afraid we'd never see you again."

"Nolan's with you?" Turning my head, I finally noticed him standing there.

"Hey," he said somewhat awkwardly. "Don't take it personally if I skip the hug."

"Don't worry, I won't," I replied, internally cringing. I was happy to see him—but not that happy.

"Jeez, what happened to you?" he asked.

"Nice to see you, too," I remarked, taken aback by his rudeness.

"Well, I mean . . . look at you!"

Pulling myself up onto my feet, I looked down and quickly became aware of why he'd asked the question. My clothes were wrinkled and dirty, my socks and shoes haphazardly put on, and my legs were covered in an assortment of bloody scrapes and bruises. I attempted to quickly run my fingers through my hair, but they got stuck in the knots. "It's been a rough day."

"Tell me about it!" Cassidy said dramatically. "Nolan and I got lost in the woods, met a king, and found out that we're now in the past! Oh, and Nolan fell in a hole."

Eyes darting to Nolan, I choked on a laugh as I exclaimed, "You *what?*"

"I didn't fall into a *hole*. I fell into a pit. There's a difference."

"King Robert pulled him out," Cassidy explained.

"King Robert? You guys met King Robert?" All the things James had told me about him swirled in my mind. *A mighty king . . . the rightful ruler of Scotland . . . enemy of England. Seen by the English as a traitor and an outlaw . . .*

"Yeah, we met him," Nolan said. "We talked quite a bit. You know, guy stuff."

Cassidy grinned as we exchanged a knowing look. "He was really nice. He gave us a ride here. Oh, and guess what? He's a redhead just like me! On the ride here he told me that I reminded him of his daughter, Marjorie. She has red hair, too."

"He has a daughter?"

"Yeah, it's kind of sad really. I asked him where Marjorie was, thinking it would be nice to meet her. He said that he didn't know. About eight years ago his wife, daughter, two sisters, and their family's loyal friend, Isabella, were all captured by the English. He hasn't seen them since."

"That's horrible!"

"I know. I can't imagine being separated from your whole family like that, wondering if you're ever going to see them again. . . ."

A thick silence fell upon our group. Instinctively, I knew we were all thinking the same thing. "We're going to get back home, Cassidy." I hoped my words were laced with enough confidence to hide the doubt inside me.

"Here you are: food, blankets, and a change of clothes." It was James. He was holding a basket of bread, roast meat, and vegetables. A container of water was tucked inside. Under his arm were a couple of rolled up cloth bundles. I was so grateful, I had to blink away tears that were pushing their way to the surface. *Keep it together, Ava.* "Tomorrow I've arranged for a tent to be set up for you. Unfortunately, that means that the only space we have available tonight is amongst the elements."

"That's okay, James," I said, grabbing the items. "I'm just so thankful for everything you've done."

"It's been my pleasure." The twinkle was back in his eyes. "Ah, I see you've found your friends. King Robert told me he'd found some unusually attired youth today."

"Oh, I'm sorry," I said, quickly remembering that I hadn't introduced my friends. "James, this is Cassidy and Nolan. Guys, this is James Douglas a.k.a. The Black Douglas. He's the one that found me and brought me here."

After everyone greeted one another; James gave us a slight bow, mounted his horse, and left for the other campsite. "I wonder why they have two campsites," I mumbled.

"Oh, I know," said Cassidy. "We asked the same thing when we arrived. The first camp is for the soldiers because it's near where the battle is going to be taking place. This camp site, hidden in a protective valley, is for the camp followers a.k.a. the smale folk."

"Yeah, James mentioned them. Who are they?"

"People who follow the army and do the tasks needed to keep the soldiers in fighting shape. So, like, the cooks that feed them and the blacksmiths that fix their armor and stuff."

"But I met a few soldiers that are staying here, too," added Nolan. "They came to fight, but arrived too late to train with the others."

"So, they're essentially the benchwarmers?" I asked.

"Yeah, pretty much. The ones I've talked with are cool guys. They showed me the big spears that the army is going to be fighting with. They are so cool! You should see them. They are super tall and really sharp!"

As Nolan praised the Scottish weaponry and armor, I felt sick. I wanted to shout out, "STOP! It isn't enough. You have no idea what's coming this way!" But I didn't. I'd promised I wouldn't say anything.

Feeling like I was about to burst, I knew there was at least one piece of information I could tell them. "Um, guys," I began, "I know where the rest of our friends are."

That night, I laid on a blanket looking up at the stars. I could feel the warmth from the fire, but it wasn't necessary. The sweltering summer day had turned into a perfect summer night. *Have there always been so many stars?* Thousands of beams of light glittered across the sky. They were spectacular! Finally not having to compete with the lights of the city, their radiant beauty became evident. The contented buzz of insects and the soft rustle of trees replaced the hum of traffic and murmur of nearby televisions that I'd grown accustomed to. It was strange and different, but I liked it.

"Ta-da!" Cassidy belted out. She was standing next to me, posing in her newly-gifted outfit.

"Shhh," Nolan whined from his place at the opposite end of the fire. "Some of us are trying to sleep."

"Sorry," Cassidy said in a hushed voice. To me she whispered, "So, what do you think?" She was wearing a long-sleeve dress that reached down to the floor. It was cinched at the waist with a long belt. In the firelight I could see it was a striking yellow color.

"It looks great Cassidy."

"Thanks," she said with a giggle. "There's a lot of things about our situation that I'm not happy with, but this dress isn't one of them. I feel like a princess!"

"Well, you look great. Of course, there's one thing I don't understand."

"What?"

"How come you get a yellow dress?" I asked, gesturing toward my tan one.

She hesitated for a minute before her voice squeaked out, "Tan is a nice color." She wasn't the least bit convincing. Whatever. It didn't really matter. I wasn't much into fashion and the yellow looked great on her. For a second, though, I wondered if they had given me the tan one because they took one look at me and thought, "That girl's basic. A plain dress for a plain girl."

Shaking the thought from my head, I gestured toward Cassidy's already rolled-out blanket, "Have a seat. I want to tell you something."

"Ooh, what is it?"

"Um . . . well . . ." starting was the hardest part, "I wanted to say, before here, back there. You know?"

A look of concern crossed her face. "Did you hit your head?"

"No, I didn't hit my head!" This conversation wasn't going well. I'd just have to spit it out. "I wanted to say I'm sorry! There, I said it."

"For what?"

"For snapping at you earlier, when we were in Dr. Keller's office. I wasn't really mad at you, I just . . ." The rest of the words caught in my throat. A part of me wanted to finish the sentence, to be fully open and honest about my emotions. But I just couldn't. Instead, I finished with a quick, "Anyway, I'm sorry."

"Apology accepted," she said with a smile. "It's ancient history. Of course, now that we can apparently time travel, I can't promise that we won't relive it again."

I laughed, relieved that she forgave me so quickly. "Thanks, Cassidy."

"Eh, no problem. You aren't the only one who's apologized to me today."

"Really? Who else?"

"Oh, it's nothing. Water under the bridge." I saw her eyes flick toward Nolan, but got the feeling that I wasn't supposed to press the questioning further.

As I laid back down on the blanket and looked up at the stars, I heard Cassidy whisper, "Ava, can I tell you a secret?"

"Uh . . . sure."

"I'm scared."

I smirked. "That's not much of a secret." *Does she really think she's been good at hiding that fact?*

"Gee, thanks . . ." she mumbled, clearly dismayed by my initial reaction. *Apparently, she does.*

"Hey, we're all scared. You just can't focus on it. Try to think of this as just another one of your traveling adventures. Pretend you're out camping with your family in Scotland and your parents paid the big bucks for a *super* authentic reenactment experience. You should be used to that, right?"

"Well," she hesitated, "no."

"Okay, so maybe your family doesn't do the whole history-experience thing. Just pretend you've all traveled to Scotland and . . ."

"No! I mean . . . I've never traveled anywhere before."

I was so confused. "But what about all the pictures on your dorm room wall and all the pins on your backpack?"

"They aren't really places I've been, just places I would like to go one day. Maybe."

"But what about camping?"

"Nope." Her voice was laced with sadness. That just wasn't going to work for me.

"Well, congratulations," I cheerfully exclaimed.

Propping herself up onto her elbows, she stared at me with confusion, "Why?"

"Because, that means this is your first adventure. The first of many more to come!"

A slow smile spread across her face and she laid back down. "Thanks, Ava."

"Hey, what are friends for?"

"Could you do me a favor, though?"

"What?"

"Could you please not tell the others?"

"Tell them what?"

"That I haven't traveled anywhere. I'd just rather that they didn't know."

The request didn't make any sense to me, but I couldn't see the harm in not telling them. "Your secret's safe with me," I assured her. Then, I did what any good friend would do: I locked away her secret in the same space I buried my own, knowing it would be safe there.

14

CASSIDY

“Is it Sunday already?” I mumbled, still in a foggy haze from my coma-like sleep. I could hear church bells ringing in the distance. Keeping my eyes closed, I pulled the blanket up higher. My body was trying to return back to its unconscious state, but the bells were clearing the cobwebs from my mind. “Winnie, I had the strangest dream. We were back in the past and we met a king. It was weird. . . .” The bells kept ringing. *Why are my legs itchy?* I lazily reached down to scratch them and felt a strange tingle on my neck. *A bug!*

With that sudden realization, my eyes flew open and I sat up with a jolt, furiously smacking away whatever creepy crawly was using my neck as a tightrope. Adrenaline coursed through my veins. My eyes darted in every direction. The campfire was dying out, soon to be replaced by the light of the sun that was barely peeking out above the eastern horizon. Looking down, I saw the source of my itchy legs was grass covered in morning dew. Apparently, in the middle of the night, I'd rolled off my blanket and had used it as a cover instead. As my heart slowed down to a normal pace, I was forced to conclude that it had been real. It had all been real. The blue sphere, the walk through the woods, the king and his army. All of it.

"Why are there bells?" Ava growled. Eyelids drooping, she looked as if she wanted to angrily attack whatever was making all the noise. Instinctively, I backed up a few inches in case she came to the crazy conclusion that it was me. She evidently wasn't a morning person and, unfortunately for her, this alarm didn't come with a "snooze" button.

"I think they're church bells."

"Church bells?" her head whipped toward me. "Here? Is it Sunday?"

"Who knows?! Yesterday morning I couldn't even tell you what year it was, let alone the day of the week."

"Where's everyone going?" she asked. Looking around, I noticed for the first time that everyone in the camp was walking away in the same direction, looking very much like a mass migration of an exotic species.

"Putting two and two together, I'm guessing they're going to church." Getting up, I started to roll up my blanket.

"Where are you going?"

"Wherever they're going. If they are going to church, I don't want to be late."

"Oh . . . well . . ." there was a slight uneasiness in her eyes, which surprised me, "do you think we're invited?"

"Uh, yeah. It's not like churches hand out formal invites. Everyone's welcome. Come on, I'll wake up Nolan."

As we walked along, the crowd grew larger and larger as more and more people joined the procession. Men, women, soldiers, camp followers; everyone came. Nolan walked with a new kind of swagger that he'd gained after receiving his tunic and leather boots. I got the feeling he enjoyed fitting in with the other men at camp.

A nice lady informed me that the church we were heading toward was called St. Ninians. As it turned out, it wasn't Sunday. It was Saturday. However, they were having a special mass (the Catholic version of a worship service) to celebrate the vigil of St. John the Baptist, the guy in the Bible who preached in the wilderness and was given the great honor of baptizing Jesus.

Remembering that he wore a leather belt around his waist, my hands instinctively reached toward the leather belt now encircling my own waist. In that moment, I felt somewhat connected to him. Here I was, out in (what I considered to be) the wilderness about to hear the good news of Jesus Christ. Then my stomach growled, reminding me that we hadn't eaten any breakfast. *What did the Bible say John the Baptist ate?* My stomach growled again. *Oh, yeah…locusts and honey!* As hungry as I was, the thought of eating bugs was absolutely repulsive. *I really hope they don't serve themed food at this vigil.*

We soon approached a stone wall encircling the church, forcing the mass of humanity through its relatively small archway. For several uncomfortable minutes, all I could see was a swirl of tunics and hair as I shoved my way in. Once people dispersed into the courtyard, though, I was finally able to breathe. Looking up, I found the source of the ringing: a large, rectangular, stone bell tower jutting up toward the sky. Instantly, I felt safe. It was the first time since coming here that I had. The entire journey so far had been one giant terrifying trip down the rabbit hole. But here, in a place built like a fortress and filled with the presence of God, I finally felt a moment of peace.

With so many people in attendance, there was no way everyone could fit inside the sanctuary. So, the service was held outside in the courtyard. I didn't mind. With the sun just beginning to warm the ground and the occasional breeze, I could have sat out there forever. Nolan also seemed to enjoy himself before service, befriending a few of the local children. Around 6 years old, they enjoyed teaching him a hand-clap game and taking turns getting piggy-back rides. It amazed me how quickly children warmed up to Nolan.

Ava, on the other hand, looked completely uncomfortable. Staying quiet, her eyes darted around nervously and her fingers kept fiddling with her necklace. It was funny, up until that point I hadn't even noticed she'd been wearing a necklace. I tried to get a look at the small charm, but she kept tucking it underneath her shirt collar.

Pretty soon, though, all my attention was focused on the service. I wasn't used to the worship style, so I had to closely watch the people around me. Stand when they stand. Sit when they sit. Pray when they pray. Simple enough.

When it was over, to my relief, I saw people handing out food. We hadn't eaten all day, and after the long walk and everything, we were all desperate for something good to eat.

"What do you think they've got in those baskets?" Nolan asked. "Sandwiches? I could go for a roast beef sandwich right about now!"

"Did they have sandwiches in the 1300's?" I asked.

"I don't know. Maybe. It's not like it's that complicated. Just stuff some food between a couple slices of bread."

"Ava," I said, jogging her out of her own thoughts, "you're tall. See if you can see what they've got in those baskets."

Raising herself up as high as she could, she observed, "I see bread."

"Yes!" Nolan cheered. "I told you it was sandwiches."

"That's not what I said."

The light in Nolan's eyes started to flicker. "What do you mean?" he asked.

"I said I saw bread. That's it. Just bread."

"That can't be it!" Nolan exclaimed, jumping up to take a look for himself. "No meat? No soup? No jam?!"

Placing a soothing hand on his shoulder, she said with a sigh, "It's bread, Nolan. Just bread."

Slumping back to the ground, the wind knocked out of his sails, he muttered, "Stupid bread."

Ava and I looked at each other, trying our best to suppress our giggles. It wasn't great news for us, either, but Nolan was being ridiculously dramatic about it. Pretty soon, a portly woman carrying a basket of bread headed our way. She took one look at Nolan's sour face, put her hands on her hips, and said, "Well now, why is the wee lad lookin' like he met the bad end of a whippin' stick?"

Giggling, I answered, "He's just hungry and was hoping for a bit more than bread to eat."

"Tsk, tsk now," she said, thumping him on the head.

"Ow!" he exclaimed, more startled than hurt.

"Today is the vigil of the great Saint John the Baptist, which is always commemorated with a fast of bread and water. Though with your attitude, you ought to get nothing at all!"

"I'm sorry," he said, "I didn't know."

"What do you mean you didn't . . ." she paused for a moment, her eyes widening with a sudden realization, "aye! You three are the new ones I've been hearing gossip about. The ones with the strange clothing."

"Yes, we are," I said. "My name's Cassidy, this is Ava, and the hungry one is Nolan."

"Well, it's a pleasure to meet you! I'm Agnes, keeper of the kitchen. It's my job to keep the soldiers stuffed like a prize heifer. Except today, that is." With that, she handed Nolan a piece of bread which he accepted with a forced smile. "Now that I know who you are," she continued, handing me and Ava our rations, "I'd like to know if you are planning to stay for a while."

My heart sank. I wasn't sure how to respond. Were we? We at least needed to stay long enough to get the others back. But what about after that? Could we even get back? With a knowing glance, Ava spoke up, "We're waiting for some friends. So . . . yes."

"Alright then, I can put you to good use!"

Stunned, Ava stuttered, "W-what?"

"You two girls would be perfect for kitchen duty." Noticing our hesitation, she exclaimed, "Don't tell me you two expected to lay around camp like the Queen of Sheba. We're preparing for battle! It's all hands to the plow if we expect to give the English a lesson in Scottish tenacity."

At that moment, a snicker escaped from Nolan. Like a lion alerted by the snapping of a twig, she spun her attention toward him. "The same goes for you, too, laddie! A young man, such as yourself, would be a perfect fit to assist Mr. Crockett in the blacksmith shop."

Nolan paled. "I don't know how to . . . you know . . . do blacksmith stuff."

"What's to know? As long as you have workin' legs and workin' arms you can sure as move his materials from one area to another. Just don't trip into the fire and you'll do just fine!" My mind immediately replayed the scene of him falling into the pit. This could be bad.

As she left to finish her deliveries of bread, a heavy silence hung in the air. Agnes was a whirlwind of a woman who had left us all utterly speechless. Slowly, Ava turned her head and said to me with a wince, "I don't know how to cook."

15

VICTOR

My legs hurt. My wrists hurt. My back hurt. Running my tongue across my teeth, I cringed. *My teeth feel fuzzy*. At that moment, I would have traded in my entire sneaker collection for a toothbrush and a warm shower. Instead, I was forced to bask in the dirt and grime that was sticking to my sweat after our uncomfortable night in Torwood.

The spiteful French soldier, Henry de . . . whatever, had figured that as we approached the Scottish army, it would be best if they could see the prisoners that the English had already managed to capture. You know—us. Therefore, instead of getting to ride on a horse (albeit uncomfortably), we were now walking behind one near the front of the procession. Our wrists bound by coarse rope; our only form of entertainment was dodging the horse droppings before we got splattered. David proved to be as bad at it as he was at playing dodgeball.

"Come on, man," I said to him as he stumbled right into a fresh one, "just think of it like you're playing one of your video games and hop over it. You should be able to do that."

Through gritted teeth, he seethed, "You play video games with your thumbs, not your legs. I'm not equipped for this!" With that, he stumbled into another one, letting out a scream of frustration.

"Negative 10 points," I said with a chuckle. He wasn't amused.

"I'm tired," Winnie whispered, looking half dazed. She'd barely spoken since we'd arrived. Honestly, I sometimes had to remind myself that she was even still there.

"Don't worry, it can't be much farther," I assured her. "Look!" I said pointing into the distance. On a rocky base, a grey, stone castle came into focus.

"Wow," David breathed, "so that's Stirling Castle." Winnie just stared at it, mesmerized.

I shrugged my shoulders. "Pretty 'whatever' if you ask me."

"Oh, and you've seen better?" David scoffed.

"Please, I've *been* to better." David and Winnie could get sentimental about the scenery all they wanted, but it didn't change the fact that we were currently being paraded through the streets like cattle. For what seemed like the 100th time, I struggled to loosen the rope bound around my wrists. *Just wait 'til I get out of here; they'll be sorry they ever did this to me!*

"We're slowing down," David noticed.

Winnie added, "Someone's coming."

Looking up, I saw a man on horseback bounding toward us. Slowing down upon arrival, he said to the knight in yellow (who we'd first met on the road), "Greetings Gilbert de Clare, honorable Earl of Gloucester. I, Philip Mowbray, Keeper of Stirling Castle, have arrived with a message for the king."

"He sounds Scottish," David whispered in my ear. "Think they'll tie him up, too?"

"I don't know," I whispered back. "They're sure not acting like it. I get the feeling they know him."

In response to the rider's request, King Edward II was summoned. Riding up on a silken black horse, he was dressed to impress in red and gold embroidered fabric over his suit of armor. Lions were emblazoned across his shield and a gold crown encircled his head of wavy brownish-blonde hair.

As soon as the rider, Philip Mowbray, saw him; he leapt off his horse and knelt down on the ground until King Edward II motioned him to rise. Scottish or not, Philip's actions made it perfectly clear which side he was on. Rising to his feet, Philip announced, "I have come bearing good news for Your Majesty." He paused for a moment, allowing a few of the knights (including our French friend) to finish gathering around. With triumph in his voice, he declared, "Although the Scottish forces have assembled their army, by the terms of the agreement made by myself and Edward Bruce, Your Majesty has arrived in time to successfully remain in possession of Stirling Castle, avoiding any need for useless bloodshed."

One would have expected this kind of news to be met with cheers or, at the very least, a smile. Instead, it was followed by heavy silence. When he finally spoke, Edward II asked, "Robert the Bruce is still at Stirling?"

Seemingly surprised by his response, Philip answered, "Yes, last night he moved his men to the New Park, south of Stirling Castle. That is why it took me so long to reach you, as I was forced to make a wide detour to avoid their forces."

As Edward II turned to look at the knights crowded around him, I caught sight of a wicked smile creeping across his lips. "Then I daresay, we mustn't keep them waiting. They came for a battle, and a battle is what we will give them."

Philip looked confused, "But Your Majesty, there is no need . . ."

Fire in his eyes, the king whipped his head toward him with the speed of a viper as he bellowed, "DON'T TELL ME THAT THERE IS NO NEED! I am Edward II, King of England and Wales! It is up to ME to decide if there is a need. Robert the Bruce is a traitor, an outlaw, and a murderer! I did not assemble my army simply to be used as leverage in your negotiations. I assembled them to put an end to Bruce—once and for all."

Philip looked visibly uncomfortable, but said nothing.

Continuing with a renewed sense of calm, Edward II said, "The real matter at hand is not *if* we will attack the Scots, but *how*. Mowbray, as Keeper of Stirling Castle, you must have some knowledge in this matter."

After swallowing a lump in his throat, Phillip replied, "Aye, I have been able to observe their preparations from the battlements of the castle. That is why I must advise you to not attempt an attack from the western woods. The paths through the forest have been barricaded and the surrounding growth is too thick for an army of your size to easily pass. Truthfully, this road you're on is the most suitable way to approach."

Turning again to his knights, the king asked, "Is there anyone here with objections to Mowbray's assessment?" Met with silence, the king continued, "Then we will continue to advance along the Roman Road. My

101

nephew, the Earl of Gloucester," he said gesturing toward Gilbert, the yellow knight, "will continue to lead the army."

At this, someone shouted, "But Your Majesty!" Looking around to see where the voice was coming from, I connected it to a well-groomed knight in blue who I, personally, thought looked a lot like the actor Joseph Gordon-Levitt (dark, meticulously-styled hair and a suave demeanor). "As Constable of England, it would be customary for *me* to lead our army into battle."

"With all due respect to the Earl of Hereford," Gilbert said in a tone that felt artificially respectful at best, "it seems also customary for the army to be led by a knight who has been loyal to the king."

The remark must have struck a nerve with fake Joseph Gordon-Levitt. His horse, having sensed his agitation, took a few steps and shook his head with a loud *neigh*. Holding back his rage, Fake-JGL (as I would now forever think of him) locked eyes with Gilbert and shot back, "If the Earl of Gloucester wishes to question my loyalty to the king, then I would encourage him to do so in a manner befitting a knight of his stature!"

"Well, if the Earl of Hereford . . ."

"ENOUGH!" It was the king this time. Immediately, the argument ended. "I have made my decision. Gilbert de Claire, Earl of Gloucester will lead the vanguard into battle." Gilbert shot his opponent a smug smile. "However, I also recognize the importance of our English customs. Therefore, Humphrey de Bohun, Earl of Hereford will also lead."

Gilbert's smile vanished. Neither party seemed happy about the king's order for them to share the position. Although they didn't verbally object, they glared at each other as if imagining what it would be like to shove the other one off his horse.

"In the meantime; Sir Henry de Beaumont, Earl of Buchan," the king said gesturing to our not-so-friendly French friend, "and Sir Robert Clifford," he said with a gesture toward a rugged-looking knight who had dressed himself like a blue and yellow checkerboard, "will lead a group of 600 men around the north side and get behind the Scots. That way, when Bruce's army runs away in fear—as such a cowardly band of traitors is bound to do—we'll be in place to show them that there is no escape from their miserable fate."

With no further objections, the king retreated to his central position in the procession, leaving the knights to go about their business. Philip

Mowbray rode back to Stirling Castle, Mr. Checkerboard and the French guy selected their 600 men to lead off in a different direction, and Gilbert and Fake-JGL stood next to each other playing an awkward version of the "Quiet Game." Everything considered, I was now starting to have a really good day.

Unable to contain my joy, I started laughing. David scolded me with a whispered, "Stop it! Are you *trying* to get us in trouble?" Suddenly curious, he added, "Wait, why are you laughing?"

"Don't you see what's going on? That Philip guy was totally uncomfortable with the king's decision to attack the Scottish army, the two guys leading the army can't stand each other, and it was suggested that Fake-JGL has already been disloyal to the king."

"Fake-JGL?"

"Oh, Fake-Joseph Gordon-Levitt. That's what I'm calling that Earl of Hereford guy."

"Why?"

"Oh, come on! He totally looks like him!"

"I mean . . . I guess. I can see it a little. Is that why you were laughing?"

How is he not following this? "No, Dude! I'm laughing because this army is falling apart! According to my dad, what a leader needs from his followers in order to be really strong, is loyalty. Something that this band of merry kidnappers is totally lacking!"

"So how does that help us?" Winnie asked, making me suddenly aware that she'd been listening this whole time.

"Because," I chuckled, "it means that our captors have cracks that are starting to form. If we want to get out of here, all we have to do is figure out which crack to push."

16

AVA

Any hope I had of losing Agnes in the crowd was squashed the instant I heard her thick Scottish brogue yell out, "Don't you spry young things be walkin' at a fox pace, now! My aging bones don't move like they used to." *Aww man, she found us.*

I didn't have anything against Agnes, per se. She seemed like a friendly (though somewhat pushy) woman. The real problem was that I didn't know how to do the things she was probably going to expect us to do. I wasn't a girl from the 1300's, who would have learned how to cook and clean from an early age. I grew up with maids and cooks. The only way I knew how to get food was to use a cell phone to order a pizza.

Catching up to us, Agnes wrapped her arm around my shoulders and said, "You three stick with me, and I'll show ya the lay of the land. I know everything there is to know about the camp and everyone in it. You'd be amazed at the stories one tells when they're bellied up to a hot bowl of soup!"

Seeing an opportunity to get some needed information, I grabbed it. "Agnes," I began, "you must have heard the stories about James Douglas."

She laughed. "Have I? Go to any tavern throughout Scotland and you'll hear a tale about the brave, fierce, and loyal friend of King Robert the

Bruce. But go to any tavern in England and you're sure to hear warnings about the terrifying Black Douglas who mercilessly defends Douglas castle. There's nothin' difficult in hearin' about James Douglas, just in knowin' which stories are true. What is it you're wonderin' about him?"

"Just . . . uh . . . what kind of a guy do you think he is?"

"You're wonderin' if you need to fear him."

Her bluntness caught me off guard, making a nod my only form of response.

"If you're not an Englishman, you have nothing to fear from Douglas."

"So . . . the scary stories about him aren't true?" I asked, relieved by what I was hearing.

"Now when did I say that? Did ya stick the bread I gave ya in your ears? I said you needn't *fear* him. The English exaggerate the stories, to be sure, but nobody except Jesus Christ is the embodiment of perfection. Douglas has certainly lashed out violently in the name of revenge; keeping the priestly confessionals occupied to be sure.

But what I'm telling you is that the Douglas I know is also a kind and loyal man. His father was imprisoned and killed by the English when he was just a young lad. Because of this, he sought out King Robert and asked to join his men. King Robert agreed. And though firstly joining to avenge his father's death, Douglas has since shown his true loyalty to Scotland and has found a good friend in the king. I daresay I'd bet the fine reputation of my food on the strength of their friendship."

Though I wasn't sure if her explanation was enough for me to completely let down my guard, I also felt that I could probably trust her judgment. As blunt as she was, she wouldn't be one to sugarcoat anything.

"Cassidy and I met the king on our way here," Nolan said. "He seemed like a pretty friendly guy."

"That he is," Agnes confirmed. "Humble too, which is a virtue I rarely attribute to the ruling class. Not like the English king, who sits up on his high horse and lets others fight his battles for him—which he'd have every right to do given his position. But not King Robert! There was once a time when he and his men were laying siege to a castle and, in order to reach it, they had to cross a moat. Well, when you're a knight packed down in iron and steel, you've every right to fear being the first one into water! Too deep, and you'd be walking into your own watery grave. Did King Robert send in one of his men to risk their life? No! Jumped right into the water himself,

106

he did! After a thing like that, it's no wonder that so many men are eager to fight beside him."

"Wow," breathed Cassidy, "it's a good thing he survived."

"Aye, King Robert has more lives than a cat! You should hear some of the tales the boys at the camp tell. He's been near death so many times, it seems only by the blessing of God that he's with us today."

The kitchens now in sight, I caught a whiff of something repulsive. Quickly covering my nose with my hands, I glared at Nolan, "Did you . . ."

"No way!" he screeched, shoving both fingers directly up his nose. "Whoever smelt it dealt it!"

Before I could give my retort, Cassidy interjected, "Come on you two, there's no way that smell just came out of one of us!"

Chuckling, and seemingly unaffected by the stench, Agnes said, "You're right about that! What you're smelling is coming from the dye shop over there."

Turning to my right, I saw people dipping clothes into huge vats of hot liquid. The clothes they pulled out were a bright yellow color—just like Cassidy's dress.

With a slight quiver in her voice, Cassidy asked, "What are they dipping those clothes into?"

Agnes boomed, "Horse urine, of course! Gives it that nice yellow color."

Stunned, all I could think was, *I'm so glad I got the tan dress!*

The rest of the day went pretty much how I thought it would go. Attempting to help Agnes make bread, I cracked egg shells into the batter, spilled flour all over the floor, and left my loaf in the oven until it became a charcoal rock better suited for use on the battlefield than on a kitchen table. There were a few things I did, though, that surprised even me. For instance, I thought I could knead dough. Turns out, I can't. A few minutes in and my soft dough turned into a sticky monster that refused to let go of my hands.

Needless to say, it didn't come as a shock when Agnes decided that I should go deliver food far *far* away from her kitchen. Handing me a basket of loaves (that were not made by me) she sent me off to feed the soldiers on the battlefield.

The last time I'd walked in the woods alone I'd been tired, hungry, and completely lost. This time was much different. In fact, it was quite relaxing. Trees shaded me from the intensity of the sun as I watched butterflies dance around vivid wildflowers. Small animals scurried in the distance, keeping me company. Scotland really was beautiful. Well . . . when I wasn't sucking in the scent of boiling horse urine.

As I reached the top of the hill, I was greeted by a stunning view of the battlefield. Like a green ocean, lay a large expanse of grass barely blemished by the occasional shrub. Familiar trees sprung up at the far end, hiding from view what I knew to be a winding river.

Looking down, I could see the Scottish army. A few men were on horseback, but most were standing in clusters holding tall, pointed sticks. Their armor looked like a mish-mash of whatever they could get their hands on. Thinking back to the sleek iron-laden army coming their way, a chill crept up my spine. *Let it go, Ava. There's nothing you can do.*

Catching my eye, was a man on a grey horse with bright red hair. *That must be King Robert.* Cassidy had given a pretty accurate description of him. Plus, he was wearing a crown (which kind of gave it away). However, watching him giving orders and checking on his troops, I got the impression that the crown was unnecessary. There was something about his presence that radiated "I am king" vibes. I couldn't quite put my finger on what it was exactly, but he definitely moved with a calm confidence.

For several moments I watched, captivated by the battle preparations. Men scurried about, readying themselves for the challenges ahead. In fact, I was so busy watching them, that I almost didn't notice the English army emerging from the road, half-hidden amongst the trees. King Robert didn't notice them either.

What's that knight doing? Separating himself from the rest of the English army, one soldier charged full speed ahead. A swirl of blue and gold, he streaked across the field and extended his spear. It took only a moment to realize who he was aiming for.

"BRUCE!" I screamed, panic welling up in my chest. *He isn't turning around. Why isn't he turning around?!* "LOOK!"

He didn't.

Logic would have told me that King Robert wouldn't be able to hear me. Logic also would have told me that I'd never get to him in time to warn him. But at that moment, I wasn't running on logic. I was running on adrenaline. I was also running down a very steep hill.

Everything around me became a blur. Momentum propelling my legs faster than my body could handle, I suddenly found myself skidding into the dirt. My bread basket flew down the hill and I felt the sharp sting of my scraped and bloody arms. But I didn't care. Quickly refocusing my eyes, I looked back to the battlefield and screamed, "LOOK OUT!"

Though I'm sure he couldn't hear me, he did finally notice the rider barreling toward him. With little time to spare, he grabbed an axe and charged. Time seemed to slow down. Frozen, the only sound I could hear was the pounding of my own heartbeat. The horses threw dirt into the air as their riders rode furiously toward each other, both men fully aware that there would only be one survivor.

The knight's long spear aimed directly at King Robert's chest. If there was a weapon that would hit first, that would be it. But King Robert didn't slow down. He just gripped the axe tightly in his hand and leaned forward.

The collision came alarmingly fast. As soon as the spear was about to hit, King Robert swerved to the side and brought the full strength of his axe upon the rider's head with such force that the rider's helmet was split in two. Then it was over. Left only with a broken axe handle in his hand, King Robert rode back to his troops.

The cheers from the Scottish side seemed distant and hollow, muffled by a *thump thump* sound pounding in my ears. Suddenly flooded with a wave of nausea, the little bit of food I'd eaten that day made an immediate resurgence.

Pale and shaky, I slumped into the dirt. Replaying the last few moments in my mind, I was consumed by a strange mixture of relief, horror, and fear. More overwhelming, though, was a feeling of utter hopelessness. Lying in the dirt, I finally allowed myself to do the one thing I tried hard never to do. I cried. All alone, I didn't bother holding back or keeping quiet. Streams of hot tears raced down my cheeks as every emotion I'd locked away was finally set free.

Exhausted, I looked up into the cloudless sky. "I can't do this," I whispered. "I'm not strong enough. I'm not brave enough." A lump caught in my throat as I choked out, "I'm not good enough." A fresh wave of tears burst from my eyes. "God, I just mess everything up! I can't save them. I can't save *anyone*! I can't even save myself."

Though painful, the honesty of my words released a weight off my chest that I hadn't been aware was even there.

I thought about getting up. I thought about gathering the basket and bread littering the ground. But instead, I just closed my eyes. *Maybe I'll lie here just a little longer.*

Though feeling somewhat refreshed after a much-needed nap, I could have done without the pounding headache. *Pull yourself together, Ava. Ugh . . . I really have to stop talking to myself in the third person.*

I managed to find where the basket had landed but abandoned the bread. Most of it had disappeared (probably at the hands of a hungry squirrel) and the rest was covered in dirt. So, without anything to give the soldiers, I made my way back up the hill.

To my surprise, I ran into Cassidy, Nolan, and a rather large group of camp followers sitting at the top. "What are you doing here?" I asked.

"Oh, hey Ava!" waved Cassidy. "Agnes let me out of the kitchen for a while to check out what's going on down there. She wants me to report back with a battle update."

"Mr. Crockett wanted to come see the skirmish for himself," Nolan said, pointing to a rugged elderly gentleman covered in soot. "I guess this is like their version of watching the Superbowl."

"Right . . ." I hesitated, yet again reliving the bloody scene I'd just witnessed. This was nothing like the Superbowl. "Is everyone okay . . . I mean . . . what's going on?"

"Well," said Nolan, "a group of the Scots are surrounded."

"WHAT?"

"But they're okay! A group of English horsemen tried a sneak attack from over there." He pointed to the left side where the church we'd been to that morning, St. Ninians, was standing. "Luckily, the Scottish spearmen formed a schiltron formation."

"A what?"

"A schiltron formation. Mr. Crockett explained that it's when a group of soldiers squeeze themselves together to form a human shield. Kind of like that," he pointed below.

Looking out once again, I saw a cluster of Scottish spearmen in the distance holding out their pointed weapons in various directions, looking very much like a human porcupine. It seemed to be working, though. As gilded knights on horseback charged at the porcupine, their horses took most of the damage, knocking their riders off with a *thud*. Once down, the Scots took care of the rest. "Their armor isn't protecting them," I said, realizing what was happening. "It's weighing them down."

"Yep," Nolan beamed, "they're getting so frustrated now, some of them are just chucking weapons hoping to hit something. Good luck with that!" He laughed.

Sitting down next to Cassidy, I tried to fully process what I was seeing. *But they protected themselves. . . .*

"Ava, what happened to your arms?" Cassidy exclaimed as she flipped my left arm over, revealing the bloody scrapes.

"Nothing," I said quickly, withdrawing my arm and pulling my sleeve down. "I just fell."

"Are you okay? It looks painful."

"Yeah, I'm fine." She looked at me for a moment, as if trying to figure out if she believed me. "Really, I'm fine," I assured her with what I hoped was a convincing smile. "Apparently, I'm not great with hills."

"LOOK! They're running away!" Nolan shouted, jumping into the air and ending any further questioning from Cassidy. Sure enough, the moving porcupine had split the English in two, sending some running north to Stirling Castle and the rest running south to seek protection from the main host of Englishmen. Cheers rang out across the hillside.

Victorious, but exhausted, the Scottish troops sat on the ground, fanning themselves with their helmets. "Come on," said a young boy sitting near us, "we ought to bring them some water." Following his lead, we helped haul several water containers down the hill.

The men, covered in sweat and dirt, were elated to receive the libation. As the troops recovered from their ordeal, you could hear the air gradually fill up with laughter and excited chatter as they soaked in the victory.

"Tis a moment of celebration," came a booming voice behind me. Turning around, I was finally face-to-face with King Robert.

I wanted to hit him and scream, "You scared the pudding out of me earlier!" But I didn't.

"You are all to be commended for your strength, bravery, and unity. Today, you showed the English what you get when you mess with the Scots!" A loud cheer rang out from the crowd. "You can be mighty sure that King Edward II will be enraged when he discovers that tonight, not one, but two of his most powerful knights on horseback were defeated by men of foot!" Again, there was another loud cheer.

"You should all be very proud," he said. The tone of his voice had suddenly changed. It was quieter and more thoughtful as he took a moment to look into the eyes of his men. "You have all proved yourselves tonight. So, if you wish to retire and go back home to your families, I leave the decision in your hands. No shame shall befall a single man here, no matter his choice."

There was no cheer this time, only contemplative silence. Finally, a man stepped forward. Middle-aged, he still had flecks of dirt and debris trapped in his beard. Beads of sweat rolled down his forehead. "Good king," he began, "command us to go into battle tomorrow. For no fear of death will cause us to fail you. Until our land is free, we will persevere!" Startled by the outcry of cheers, I looked around. All the men looked different. Different ages, different hair colors, different heights. But they all had the same eyes. Eyes filled with determination.

Upon seeing this, King Robert hesitated slightly before simply saying, "Sirs, since that is your wish, be ready in the morning." Then he mounted his horse and rode away.

17

WINNIE

"I can't believe he did that," David mused. "What was he thinking?"

"Probably of glory," Victor replied. "Could you imagine if he'd succeeded? He would have taken out the Scottish leader with one fail swoop!"

Earlier that day, we'd had a front row seat to the most gruesome attack I'd ever had the misfortune of witnessing. One of the English knights had tried attacking Robert the Bruce all by himself. It hadn't ended well.

After the brutal defeat, we were separated from the soldiers and taken into the woods where camp was being set up. David, Victor, and I were now sitting on the ground, tied to the rear wheel of a large wooden cart. Leaning against the side of it, I pulled my knees to my chest, wrapped my arms around my legs, and rested my chin on my knees. A human ball.

Unlike my fellow prisoners, I didn't feel much like talking. A deep sadness weighed heavy on my chest. If it hadn't been for the serious dehydration I was experiencing, I probably would have started crying again. I just wanted to go home. I wanted to see my mom again, hug her and never let go.

I wish I hadn't lost the book. I was haunted by the knowledge that the book I'd borrowed from Dr. Keller's office had been lost when we were sucked through the swirling blue vortex. *Maybe there was something in there that could have gotten us out of this mess. If only I'd held onto it tighter!* But I hadn't. I'd let it go. It was all my fault. There was nothing I could do now except listen to the voices around me.

"Did you notice what he was wearing?" David asked.

Victor snorted, "No, I guess I missed that episode of *Medieval Project Runway*."

"He was wearing the same coat-of-arms that Humphrey de Bohun was wearing."

"Who?"

"The Earl of Hereford."

"Who?"

David sighed, relinquishing any hope of using the knight's correct name, "Fake-JGL."

"*Oh*," Victor said with a newfound understanding, "Joseph Gordon-Levitt's brother from another mother. One of the guys leading the army. Got it! Why didn't you just say that?"

David took a deep, restraining breath. "Okay, but did you notice it?"

"Notice what?"

"THE OUTFIT!"

Clearly amused by David's outburst, Victor laughed, "No, I didn't. Was it on the 'Hot' or 'Not' list? I hear showing up to a battle in the same outfit is a major faux pas!"

David playfully kicked his shoe, "Cut it out! That's not what I mean!"

I thought David could use some help. Lifting my head up, I tried to raise my voice a bit so they could hear me. "It shows that the knights are probably related."

The boys both stopped talking and stared at me. *Was it something I said?*

"Yeah," David finally said, "that's what I was getting at. And Humph . . . Fake-JGL looked really angry."

"Now that you mention it, I did notice that," Victor agreed. "He had a look on his face kind of like, well, that guy." He pointed a finger at the newly-arriving Sir Robert Clifford.

Eyes glowing with anger, Clifford flung himself off his horse, marched over to a metal kettle that was sitting by the fire, and kicked it as hard as he could. "Ahhhhhhhh!" he screamed, fists clenched so tightly his knuckles turned white.

I dug my heels into the dirt and used them to press myself as hard as I could against the wooden cart. I was hoping for invisibility, but knew my attempts were futile.

"Yeah, kind of like checkerboard guy," Victor confirmed, completely void of fear.

"Don't you know any of their names?" David asked.

"What does it matter?"

"Shhhhh," I silenced them. The French knight, Henry de Beaumont, was arriving and looked just as angry. Unlike Clifford, though, he managed to keep his composure.

"Ahhhhhhh!" Clifford screamed again, throwing his helmet to the ground.

Henry quickly walked up behind him and grabbed his arm. "Not here," he said sternly, cautiously eyeing the incoming soldiers. With that, the two knights stormed off together.

"Weren't those two supposed to be attacking the Scottish army as they *retreated?*" David asked.

Victor shrugged, "Guess that didn't pan out." Indeed, the only reason for such a scene would be if something had gone wrong. Horribly wrong.

Hearing hushed voices, I strained my ears, struggling to understand what was being said. I couldn't quite make it out, but the voices were coming from the other side of the cart. Quietly, I slid underneath. David and Victor were too distracted by all the commotion to even notice my absence.

The dark underbelly of the cart gave me a slight sense of security as I shimmied my way toward the light on the other side. My eyes zeroed in on several pairs of feet clustered together. The ropes tied around my wrists became taught and impeded my progress, but I was at least close enough to hear what the men were saying.

"They said the Scots would retreat in fear," one man whispered. "Instead, a seasoned knight, the likes of Sir Robert Clifford, has been driven away from the field by a handful of footmen!"

"Don't forget," said another, "that two of our strongest warriors were taken. One by the Scots, and the other by death! How is it that we've been made to march all the way here from England, only to be *humiliated?* We're 10 times stronger and more powerful than them, yet we're the ones running like a dog with his tail between his legs!"

A third man spoke up. His voice trembled, "Don't you see? When our Lords wage an unrighteous war, God is offended and brings misfortune. I fear there is more misery to come, as we should have made peace with Scotland long ago."

Abruptly, their voices stopped. Thick boots plodded toward them.

Afraid to get caught by whoever had frightened them into silence, I cautiously inched backwards. Slow at first, my exodus was quickly sped up by a strong tug at my rope. Yanked out from beneath the dark, dusty underbelly of the cart, I abruptly came face-to-face with a bearded stranger.

I couldn't move. I couldn't think. Like a deer caught in the headlights of an oncoming car, there was no escaping my fate. All I could squeak out was, "Hi."

"What were you doing down there?" he asked with a Scottish brogue.

"W-w-well . . ."

Lowering his voice to that of a whisper, he leaned in, "Doin' a bit of eavesdroppin' were we? Or planning an escape?"

"I-I-I wasn't trying to escape, honest." That part was true.

"Good," he said firmly, leaning back and taking a seat on the ground next to us. "Because the wrath of the English isn't somethin' you're bound to forget." Though his words could have been taken as a threat, I got the impression they were more of a gentle warning. Realizing that he wasn't going to hurt me anytime soon, I cautiously pulled my stomach off the dusty ground and eased into a sitting position.

"So, what are you? Our babysitter?" Victor asked.

"Only for a moment. As the Earl of Buchan is otherwise engaged, he sent me over to make sure the three of you were all still here."

David leaned over and whispered to Victor, "The French guy."

"Imagine my surprise when I found only the two of ya! What was it you were doin' under there little lady? You said you weren't escapin', but were ya eavesdroppin'?"

"Um . . ." not having the heart to lie, I lowered my gaze.

"It's alright," he said with a warm grin, "anyone with any sense already knows what's being said over there as well as in a hundred other spots around this camp. The beatin' they took today is not one to be taken lightly."

"You keep saying 'they' or 'the English,'" David observed. "Aren't you one of them?"

The stranger ran his hand though his greying locks of dirty-blonde hair and sighed. "Well now, it is true that I fight for them. But Scotland is my homeland."

"So, you're a traitor," Victor said bluntly.

David's eyes bulged and I readied myself to dive back under the cart if need be.

The stranger, on the other hand, didn't look the least bit bothered. "To some," he replied matter-of-factly.

"And that doesn't bother you?" Victor asked.

The stranger gazed off into the distance, worry lines deepening as he became drawn into his thoughts. "It's not that simple. I live in southeastern Scotland where our lands are vulnerable to English raids. In my days, I've seen many a village burn for standing against Edward II and his father, the late King Edward I. I love my country, truly I do, but I have a wife and a family to protect. Should I turn against England, I cannot guarantee their safety."

Moments ago, I'd been terribly afraid of the stranger. Now, I just felt pity for him. I understood the grip of fear, probably better than most. I'd often wished that I could be brave and bold like the heroes in the books I read. Yet, even as dreams of grandeur swirled in my head, a voice inside would quickly remind me that I wasn't brave at all. I just wasn't the type of person that could ever do stuff like that.

Leaning forward, I gently placed my hand on his shoulder. Startled, he looked my way, revealing a slight watery sheen to his eyes. But with a single blink, it was gone.

Awkwardness crept through my body. "I'm sorry about your family," I said, then quickly sat back, hoping nobody was staring at me.

"Thank you," he said with sincerity.

"So, you don't like the English?" Victor asked.

Quickly looking around to make sure he wouldn't be overheard, he whispered, "No, I do not. They are vile thugs to whom this land does not rightfully belong. Edward I was a man whose veins pulsed with the heartbeat of revenge. Not even the church of England could stop his violent pursuits. His son, on the other hand, is weak-willed and frivolous. He cares neither for politics nor war, but only for ways to amuse himself. There's only but a few nobles in the kingdom that truly respect him."

"Then why fight at all?" David asked. "Why not go back to England? By the rules of the deal, they had already won."

"Aye, they did. It's rather a hard thing to know what goes on inside a person's heart. Though if I were to guess, I'd say the king has something to prove. Living in the shadow of one's father is a terrible place to be. Besides, a man can only get poked so many times with a thistle before he has a strong desire to pull it out of the ground."

"But you don't," Victor said.

"What do ya mean?"

"I mean, the English keep attacking your land and your people. Yet, you still fight beside them. I understand that you want to protect your family, but how safe are they going to be with England in power?"

Victor's words were unsettling. I wasn't used to hearing someone talk so openly. However, despite my discomfort, I had to admit that he had a point. It sounded as if the stranger's family would be in danger either way.

Again, running his hands through his hair, the bearded stranger fell silent. Several long minutes passed before he blurted out, "You're right."

"I am?" Victor asked in surprise, then realized he'd momentarily lost his cool factor. "I mean . . . I know I am."

"I've lived my life as a coward, fearing retaliation from the powerful. All the while, fighting to keep those very souls in power." With newfound urgency, he leapt to his feet. "I have to fix this. I have to warn him."

"Warn who?" asked David.

The stranger's eyes darted around the camp, in search of unwanted ears. Then, they locked with David's. "You know who." Lowering himself back to our level, he whispered, "He does not know the true weakness within the camp and must be warned."

"But how? Are they really going to just let you get up and walk out? I mean . . . they don't seem to have a shortage of rope around here." David held up his wrists to showcase Sir Henry de Beaumont's handiwork.

As a look of doubt crept onto the stranger's face, a smug smile crawled over Victor's. "I have an idea. What you need is a distraction."

Still unsure, the stranger asked, "What kind of a distraction?"

Victor winked. "Untie us and you'll find out."

Uh-oh. What is he going to do? Wait a minute . . . what are WE going to do?! I don't like where this is going. We're just kids! We've been warned about the wrath of the English. What will they do to us?! Voices of fear screamed in my head. I looked at Victor. He seemed ready to burst with the anticipation of causing chaos. I looked at David. A momentary nervousness was covered up with an agreeable nod and a smile. They were both crazy! There was no way I was going to . . .

Then I looked at the stranger. He seemed touched, moved by the willingness of others to help him, even if it meant putting themselves at risk. I instantly felt ashamed. Ashamed that I was such a selfish coward. The stranger had also been afraid, yet he was now about to make a different choice. A choice to be brave. If he could change then maybe, just maybe, I could, too.

"Alright," he said, "I will under one condition: that you tell me your names. For should one day someone ask who aided me in my time of need, I should very much like to tell them."

"I'm Victor."

"And I'm David."

The boys beamed and the stranger reciprocated with a warm smile. Then he looked at me. "And what name has been adorned upon this valiant lass?"

Embarrassed, my cheeks turned hot. "Winnie," I said.

"It is an honor," he replied with a bow of his head.

"What's your name?" David asked.

The stranger smiled, "Alexander."

"Nice to meet you, Alexander," Victor said. Excitement bubbling within him, he held up his wrists, "Now, let's do this!"

18

AVA

"Oh, hush your wimperin'! You sound like a drowning cat!" Holding out my wounded arms, Agnes had splashed an unknown liquid onto them that burned like fire!

"Well, it hurts," I protested.

"Then you ought to try keepin' on your feet next time!" Grabbing hold of one of my wrists, she quickly spun a strip of cloth around the wound and secured it tightly before doing the same to the other. I didn't want to complain, but her bedside manor could have used some serious work.

"There," she said, finishing with the second arm, "you're all taken care of. A pretty young girl, such as yourself, need take better care! There's no sense in hidin' the beauty God's given you under a pile of wrappings." She shook the extra cloth strips in the air to highlight her point before turning to go put them away.

Pretty? Beauty? All understandable concepts, to be sure, but I couldn't remember ever having heard them directed toward me. Sure, I'd occasionally get a "you look nice," or a "that outfit really suits you," or a million other phrases to compliment a person who'd never be on the cover of Vogue. But *pretty?* It felt strange to hear, yet . . . kind of nice.

"Course I hope you didn't go bleedin' on the bread I gave ya," Agnes said, snapping me away from my thoughts. "I'd hate for the men to be talkin' poorly about me bread!"

"Uh . . . no . . ." I hesitated, remembering that I hadn't actually delivered any.

Agnes spun around, "You did deliver the bread, didn't ya?" Was she a mind reader? Nothing got past this woman!

"So, about the bread . . ."

Agnes strode across the room, hands on her hips. Thrusting my chin up, she squeezed my cheeks together with one of her large hands, making me look like a bug-eyed fish. "Look me in the eyes and curb a lying tongue! Did you deliver the bread?"

Lips puckered, I mumbled, "No."

Agnes released my cheeks from her death grip and wagged a finger in my face, "Do you believe to be the only one needin' to eat?"

"No."

"Those boys are on the frontline fightin' for our independence. The least we ought to do is feed them!" She grabbed a basket, tossed in several loaves, and shoved it into my hands. "You best get to goin'!"

"Now? It's getting dark!"

"Then you'd best hurry."

It was a battle I knew I wasn't going to win.

Setting off toward the wooded hillside, I watched as the sun sank lower into the sky. It wouldn't be long before it disappeared completely.

"Where are you going?" came a voice next to me. It was Nolan.

"To the battlefield."

"Now?!"

"I have to deliver bread."

"I thought you already did that."

"You would have thought . . ." I muttered under my breath.

"Want some company?"

"Sure. Why not?" I'd tried to sound nonchalant about it, but secretly I was thankful for his presence. Considering the number of armed people running around, traveling in a pair seemed like a pretty good idea.

"So, how's working for Agnes?" he asked.

I shot him a look.

He laughed, "That good, huh? If it makes you feel any better, Mr. Crockett had me lifting heavy metal in the blazing heat of the blacksmith shop for hours. My body feels like it's been hit by a Mack truck!"

I smirked. "It does make me feel better, thank you."

"Wow! Getting pleasure out of my suffering. That's cold, Ava." His fake, hurt look made me chuckle.

"That's me all right, cold as ice."

"Yeah, why is that?"

I turned to him, puzzled by the question. *Is he seriously calling me out right now?* I'd meant what I'd said as a light-hearted joke. "What are you getting at?" I asked.

"Oh, come on," he said with a cavalier attitude, "you know how you are."

Now I was getting irritated. "No, Nolan, how am I?"

"You know," he gestured towards me, "icy. Cold. You get all serious and put up like a billion layers of ice to keep people away from you."

"I do not!"

"Oh really?" He stopped and turned to me. "Then how come when I asked you about the letter you found in the laboratory, you stopped talking and walked away?"

"Maybe I just don't like talking to you."

"Okay, fair enough. But if that's the case, then why doesn't anybody know why you're at Providence?"

The question caught me momentarily off guard. "What?"

"Why are you at Providence? I mean, everyone already knows you're a criminal. It's not like it's some big secret." My jaw dropped, shocked by his forwardness. "Yet, nobody knows what you did, where you're from, or why you got sent here. I asked Cassidy, and even she doesn't know."

"You asked Cassidy?" I felt betrayed. *They were talking about me behind my back?*

"You came up in conversation. But Cassidy said she didn't know anything. Which just goes to show that it isn't only me you don't want to talk to. It's everybody."

My face flushed hot. All words seemed insufficient for the rage that burned within. Attempting to restrain my emotions, I stoically said, "Go back to camp. I can walk by myself." I turned on my heels and marched farther into the woods.

"Oh, come on, Ava," he said, "don't be like that!"

I kept walking.

"See, this is what I mean," he yelled after me, "you keep putting up walls!"

That was it. That was the last straw. Fire in my eyes, I stormed back to where he was standing and unleashed my wrath. "FINE, NOLAN, FINE! WHAT IS IT YOU WANT TO KNOW? You want to know what Maci was getting at with her little letter? I'll give you a hint . . . I'M A CRIMINAL! Yes, Nolan, I'm a criminal. But according to you, everyone already knows that. Of course, I sort of figured that from all the stares and passive aggressive comments I've received *en masse* since arriving at Providence. Yet, apparently, you all want to know more! Okay, sure. I'm an open book. You want to know my favorite color? It's red. My favorite animal? Polar Bears. How about my favorite movie? It's a tough call, but I'd have to go with *The Goonies*. I'm a sucker for adventure stories."

Nolan was frozen, completely confused and unsure of what to do.

I wasn't finished. I was just getting started. My voice became quiet, yet menacing. "But that's not really what you want to know, is it? Those aren't the kind of things that make a person interesting. Not interesting enough to gossip about. No, the only reason you and your little friends want me to 'open up' is because you want to know all about my dark past. Okay, I'll play along. What is it you want to know? Want to know what it's like to be handcuffed and thrown into the back of a squad car? That's always fun. Oh, or how about the moment when you realize that everyone in your life would rather talk *about* you than *to* you?"

I took a step forward, my gaze never faltering. "Or maybe you want to know what it feels like when your father doesn't even look at you like you're his kid anymore." I shouldn't have spoken those words. Pain I'd thought I'd successfully repressed pounded at my heart.

"Ava," Nolan finally spoke up, "I didn't mean to upset you. I just wanted to . . ."

"What?" I cut him off, unwilling to let him finish whatever lame excuse he was going to come up with. "You just wanted to what? Find out what it is I did? That's the million-dollar question, isn't it?"

The resulting silence was palpable. I looked into his eyes and smiled, a sad smile, knowing I was right. I took a deep breath and let it out. "Well, it's none of your business."

I backed away a few steps, ready to leave, but stopped and added, "By the way, if you're wanting me to tell you what I did, in the hopes that it wasn't so bad; or as proof that I'm not as screwed-up a person as everyone thinks I am. Well . . ." I swallowed a lump in my throat, "I can't do that."

Having said my peace, I turned around and left. In the distance, I heard Nolan call out, "Ava, wait! Come back!"

I didn't.

19

AVA

I'd traveled hundreds of years into Scotland's past, yet still wasn't free of my own. When the judge had laid down his sentence, I'd thought I'd escaped imprisonment. I was wrong. From where I stood, all I could see was a life sentence. The thought was enough to make me just keep on walking and never come back. *Wait, why do I have to go back?* My mother was dead, my father hated me, and my sisters were actively distancing themselves from me. They'd even gone so far as to block me from their social media accounts. If I was bound to receive the same treatment from the kids at Providence, then why return? Sure, the lack of modern conveniences was a bit problematic (I really missed toilet paper), but maybe staying here was truly the only way of getting a fresh start.

So distracted by the battle that raged inside, I didn't notice the consuming darkness until a tree branch smacked me across the face. The constant forest abuse was a bit repetitive for my liking, but it did awaken me to the realization that for the last several minutes, I hadn't been aware of where I was going.

Sounds grew louder. The crunch of the forest floor, the fluttering of heavy wings, the scuttering of small creatures. The freedom I'd once felt from being alone morphed into fear. *Don't panic*, I told myself, *you can figure this out. What do they say to do when you're lost? Hug a tree. Ugh, which only works if someone is looking for you. Never mind. Moss grows on the . . . east side of a tree? North side of a tree? I can't remember! Does it matter, Ava? You can't see the moss anyway. Think!*

I spun around, looking for any clue that would point me in the right direction. Then I felt it. The gradual slope of the ground beneath my feet. I'd been walking uphill for most of the journey. If I followed the slope downhill, I should either end up at my target destination on the other side, or else I'd end up back where I started. A win either way!

The slope was gradual at first, but soon increased dramatically. I quickened my pace, moving as fast as I could without doing another faceplant. To my relief, it wasn't long before I saw a faint light escaping from the confines of a tent. I'd found the campsite! Gripping my basket of bread, I thought, *After all this, they'd better not tell me they're gluten free!*

Like a moth to a flame, I wanted nothing more than to enter the illuminated tent, but froze when I heard a loud voice from within.

"We can't risk it!" the voice boomed. "Scotland has but only one army. Should we be defeated tomorrow, Scotland would never be able to recover."

I took a step back from the door, unsure of what to do. I didn't want to interrupt whatever was going on inside, but I also didn't want to walk away. Curiosity had cemented my feet to the ground.

Another man spoke up, "So what do you suggest? That we run away? Our loyalty is to Scotland, which is why we should stay and fight!"

The first one responded, "Have I ever before backed down from a fight? Has there ever been a moment when I've hesitated from giving my life for the cause? What I'm talking about is not disloyalty or cowardice. It's about thinking what's best for the future of Scotland. What do you think will become of our people if they are left without an army to fight for them? Left without a king to lead them? Their fate will be sealed!"

The second man spoke up again, "And what is the purpose of an army if not to fight? We have the chance to finally put an end to English tyranny once and for all! Did you not see what happened on the battlefield today? By the grace of God, our footmen took two of their finest knights!"

"And how many more await us?!"

"ENOUGH!" came a commanding voice. Silence.

Heart pounding in my chest, I feared that any slight noise or movement would carry through the air and alert them to my presence. The commanding voice spoke again, "I have heard your concerns, and there is much to consider. If you'd be so kind as to leave me for a few moments, I shall have my decision within the hour."

Hide! Quickly pressing myself against the side of the tent, I blended into the shadows. Luckily for me, as the group of men exited the tent, their agitated mutterings and inner turmoil seemed to distract them just enough for me to remain unseen.

Just as I was about to walk away unnoticed, I heard, "You can come in now." I stopped. *Surely, he's not talking to me.* "Are you going to stand outside my tent eavesdropping all night, or are you going to come in?" *Rats!*

Sheepishly, I pulled open the flap and stepped inside. King Robert Bruce sat in the center of the room, elbows resting on a wooden table, candlelight illuminating the deep worry lines etched into his face. "Have a seat," he said.

Bracing myself for the worst, I remained standing and began to plead my case. "I wasn't eavesdropping, Your Highness. I mean, I was, but that wasn't why I was here. I brought bread, see?" I lifted up the basket as Exhibit A. "But then I heard talking and I didn't want to interrupt."

"Ava, have a seat." This time I obliged. His demeanor was stoic, his feelings unreadable.

"How do you know my name?" I asked.

With a vague smile he said, "I find it's often a good idea to know who's in my camp. Just as I often find it's a good idea to know who's listening at my door."

"Robert . . . Your Highness, I really didn't . . ."

He held up a hand, "It's alright. I believe you meant no harm." My shoulders relaxed, loosed from their bonds of fear. "Besides, all you've heard tonight will soon be known in the morning. All that remains is my final decision."

"Oh, alright. Well, I'll just leave you to it then."

Thanking my lucky stars that I'd be able to get out without serious punishment, I turned to go when I was stopped by, "Ava, wait just a moment." *So close, and yet so far!* I slowly turned back to face him.

"Yes?"

"Do I not get any bread?"

I laughed out loud and handed him the basket, taking the seat he'd offered me earlier.

He picked out a couple slices and handed me one. "There's nothing so good as Agnes' fresh-baked bread!"

"It is really good," I had to admit. It was so much tastier than the pre-packaged sliced bread I normally ate. "It's one of the good parts about being here."

"Why are you here?"

I about choked. "What do you mean?"

"I met your friends, Cassidy and Nolan. James told me that you all are from the land of Providence, but that you need to help three of your friends escape from the English before you can return."

"That's right."

"But what I'm curious about is, why did you come to Scotland to begin with? Many have come to fight for our cause, but your friends didn't even know who I was. Aren't you all a bit young to be away from your homeland?"

He was right, of course, but I didn't think that tales of a time-traveling ball would help our case, so I decided to leave out the details. "We all go to school together, but ended up getting lost when we went out exploring. If I can figure out how to help our other friends escape, then I can try to figure out how to get them back."

"What about you?"

"What about me?"

"You said how to get *them* back. Don't you want to go home too?"

"Oh . . ." sweat dampened my palms, "sure. Maybe. Would it be bad if I stayed?"

"Of course not! You'll find the Scots are a welcoming lot, though sometimes a bit stubborn."

I laughed. "Then I'm sure I'd fit right in!"

"I'm sure you would, lass. But won't your family worry about ya?"

I lowered my gaze, "They won't miss me."

"I see." I heard the creak of his wooden chair as he shifted his weight. "Did ya do somethin' you're not proud of?"

Stunned and horrified, I snapped my eyes upward. *How did he know? How did everybody know?*

"I'll take that as a 'yes,'" he said.

"How did you know?"

"Because the guilt and shame you feel are written across your face."

I felt angry and emotionally exposed. I thought about getting up and storming out of the tent right then and there. But the next thing he said stopped me in my tracks.

"I can read it quite easily because, for years, it was what I saw whenever I caught my own reflection."

"You did something bad?"

"Aye."

"What did you do?"

"It was my fault a man lost his life, and not on the battlefield."

"Oh . . ." I hadn't been expecting that.

"Me and this other man both had claim to the throne of Scotland. A throne that was being withheld from us while Edward I, King of England, was still alive. When Edward fell ill, we made a deal. Upon his death, one of us would get the crown in exchange for the other man's estates. I'd trusted him to keep our agreement confidential. However, when Edward made a surprising recovery, he exposed our plan to the king. I narrowly escaped with my life.

"Furious at the betrayal, I confronted him." Robert paused. His face was pulled back from the light, making it hard to see, but the jovial spirit he'd had but a moment ago, was gone. "After the fight, I was a wanted man. I spent much of my time on the run, living in the woods and fearing the wrath of the English and the vengeance of the man's family. Though I have as yet been able to run from the people who hunt me, I know I can never be successful at running from God.

"He saw what I did. The guilt from my actions tormented my spirit. I begged for forgiveness. I pleaded for absolution, but felt as if I hadn't received it. Then one day, I realized that it wasn't God who was withholding forgiveness. . . . It was me. I know that our God is a merciful God. I know that when we ask for His forgiveness, it is separated as far from us as the east is from the west. Yet, I hated what I'd done so much, that I'd rejected this free gift." Robert leaned in toward the light and looked into my eyes. "Are you, too, rejecting His gift, Ava?"

A lump caught in my throat. I couldn't speak. I grabbed hold of my necklace, like a child gripping a security blanket.

"That's a lovely necklace," he said.

I looked down at the small, gold cross between my fingers. "Thank you," I whispered. "My mother gave it to me."

131

"Did she tell you about Jesus?"

I nodded, tears welling up in my eyes as I thought of her.

"Then you know that all you have to do is ask Him for forgiveness of your sins, no matter what they are, and He will forgive you."

"But nobody else will. It doesn't matter what I do, people won't let me forget what I've done. You're lucky, everyone loves you. I hear them around camp. They say you're a hero! All anybody sees of me is a criminal!"

For some odd reason, Robert's smile returned to his face. "Do you know what the English call me?"

I shook my head.

"The Outlaw King."

"Really?"

"Aye, I daresay that tales of my fall from grace will stand the test of time."

"And that doesn't bother you?"

He leaned over and picked up his crown that was resting on a small table. "You see this crown? For a long time, I fought for this crown. It was withheld from my grandfather, despite our royal lineage, and placed onto the heads of those who should not rule. I spent years and sacrificed much to get it back. Now that I have it, I can feel its full weight. The responsibility that comes with this crown, at times, is crushing. Even worse is the daily reminder that I am not now, nor have I ever been, a perfect man. I often feel unworthy to lead my people. But what strengthens me is the knowledge that I am not truly their king."

"What?!" *Did he just say what I thought he said?*

"Don't twist my words, now, Ava. I am the King of Scotland. But I am only a temporary king, placed into this position by one who is much greater than I. You see, Christ is the true king. He is the ruler of the universe. And it is not this crown, nor my bloodline, that makes me royal. It is because Christ adopted me as his own son, that truly makes me royalty. It is what makes you royalty, too."

"Me?" The thought of me being anything even close to royalty felt strange. After all, I was far more comfortable in sneakers and jeans than I would be in a ballgown and tiara.

"Yes, you. God, the King of the Universe, had adopted you as His daughter. So even though the world around you may never forgive you, you need not worry about that. Because as both children and subjects of the True King, we need only be concerned with trying to do His will and not ours. And if it is the True King who has pardoned you, then nothing and no one else need be of concern."

"That's it? That's all I have to do?"

"That's it." He wrapped the cloth over the remaining pieces of bread and pushed the basket over to me. "Though I think you'll find that when you start focusing on pleasing the True King with your actions, that there will be others who eventually see you for who you really are."

20

VICTOR

"What's the plan?" David asked, looking over at me expectantly.

What I had wasn't so much a plan, as it was a goal: distract. I quickly searched the immediate area, taking inventory of what we had to work with. Whatever distraction we came up with was going to have to be big! Big enough to draw every eye in the camp away from Alexander's defection.

The cart immediately caught my eye. Loaded with supplies for the camp, it was almost certain to have something of use. "Cover me," I said to Winnie and David, motioning for them to scoot in front of me. Alexander had already untied our ropes, so our captivity was now only a façade, buying us a few extra minutes to prepare for whatever was going to come next.

Keeping low and out of sight, I cautiously sneaked over to the back of the cart and climbed inside. *What do we have here? Grain? Not helpful. Cloth? Maybe, but probably not. Barrels of water?* They would be useless for the plan, but I was really thirsty. Leaning against the barrels were a few leather canteens. I picked one up, removed the cork, and prepared to take a sip when my nose drew in a sharp odor. *This isn't water!* Momentarily disappointed, I replaced the cork and was about to toss it aside, when the lightbulb inside my head went on. *Now this is something we can use!* After checking to make sure the contents of the barrels were the same as the contents of the canteens, I set to work loosening the small plugs in the side of each barrel. The pungent liquid seeped out the sides and pooled onto the cart's wooden floor. Grabbing one of the canteens, I leapt off the cart and crawled over to my friends, shoving the canteen behind Winnie's back before anyone at camp could see it.

Startled by my actions, she was about to say something before the panicked look in my eyes clamped her mouth shut. Only a moment after I'd sat down and hurriedly wrapped the rope around my own wrists, did one of the English knights walk past us. He gave us a suspicious glance before continuing on his way. Heart rate slowly decreasing, I breathed a sigh of relief.

"So," David began, excitement in his eyes, "what did you find?"

Once I was sure we were alone, I slid the canteen out from behind Winnie's back and handed it to him.

He just looked at it, unsure of what to make of my find. "Open it," I commanded.

Unplugging the cork, he took a big whiff and wrinkled his nose. "What is that?"

David passed it over to Winnie who also breathed it in. She looked up knowingly, "It's alcohol."

"Yes," I said, "and unlike water, it's flammable." As they exchanged concerned glances, I leaned in and whispered, "Here's the plan . . ."

All caught up to speed and ready to accept the consequences, it was time for action. David plugged his nose as I kicked off my shoes and removed both my socks. "Think fast," I said as I tossed him my wallet. He spastically tried to catch it, but it smacked him square in the face. *Butterfingers.*

"What am I supposed to do with this?" he asked.

"I don't know! Put it in your pocket or your own sock. I don't care. I'm workin' here!" With a look of disgust, David slid it into his pocket. I hurriedly refocused, but for the life of me, I couldn't comprehend why carrying a wallet in my sock freaked the little dude out so much.

Grabbing a few stones off the ground, I poured them into one of my socks, giving it a decent throwing weight. Then I stuffed the rock-filled first sock into the second sock and tied up the open end. Almost finished, I grabbed the canteen of alcohol and poured a little on the rounded end (careful not to get any on the section I would be holding onto). It was time.

"Are you ready?" I asked Winnie and David. They nodded. While it was evident that they were still nervous, they were carrying themselves with more strength and determination than I had ever seen. We all knew that this plan could go really bad really quickly, but they weren't going to let that stop them. I couldn't help but look at them with newfound respect. "On the count of three. One . . ." I gripped the sock tightly, "two . . ." I uncrossed my legs and positioned my feet directly under me, "THREE!"

Winnie, David, and I took off running in three separate directions. I headed straight for the fire. Honed in on the orange blaze, I didn't bother to turn around and look at the source of a loud, "HEY!" A few seconds later, (out of the corner of my eye) I could see a large figure running toward me. *Almost there!*

Right at the edge of the blaze, a meaty hand wrapped around my left arm. "Oh no you don't!" the figure shouted. But before he could completely pin me down, I whipped the sock in my right hand through the fire and, with one swift motion, lobbed it at the cart. A small fire shone upon the sock. *Come on . . .* I pleaded.

It sailed through the air like a fiery comet before landing smack dab in the middle of the cart. Within half a second, there erupted a blazing inferno. "OH YEAH!" I shouted, pumping my right arm in the air, "TOUCHDOWN!"

Shouts were heard throughout the camp as men scrambled to find buckets of water to extinguish the blaze. In the meantime, their efforts were impeded by stampedes of horses running this way and that around the campsite, braying in agitation. *That a girl!* Apparently, Winnie had successfully made it to the area where the horses were tied up. Well, *had been* tied up.

"What's happen . . ." I heard the French guy start to say as he stormed out of his tent. He didn't get to finish his sentence before crashing to the ground with a loud *clank*. Also in a hurry to get out of the tent, Mr. Checkerboard ended up tripping over French guy with a *clank, clank, clank*.

I burst out laughing as I watched the two furious knights struggle to get up under the weight of their armor. David also laughed, still holding the end of the rope he'd used to trip them. What the English had used to bind us, we'd used against them. Tying one end to a tent pole, and pulling on the other, was all it took to take those two bullies down. It felt great!

Sadly, the joy was short-lived. As soon as the two fumbling knights heard David's laughter, he became a duck in a shooting gallery. "Get him!" the French guy screamed, pointing at David.

Sobering quickly, David ran for it! He managed to dive past a few good attempts at capturing him, but his luck eventually ran out. They dragged him over to where I was being held. It wasn't long before Winnie also joined our team of captured rebels.

Though I wasn't looking forward to our upcoming punishment, I couldn't help but smile. That's because I knew that among all the chaos, I was the only one who had noticed Alexander slip away into the shadows of the woods.

"WHY YOU LITTLE . . ." Mr. Checkerboard roared as he drew his arm into the air, ready to smack David with all the strength he could muster. David turned his face, readying himself for the blow that never came. To my relief (and I'm sure David's), someone grabbed Mr. Checkerboard's arm in midair. It seemed a bold move since the rescuer was a good head shorter than the attacker.

Mr. Checkerboard turned on the man with fire in his eyes. "Aymer," he seethed, "let go of my hand." He yanked his arm away from Aymer's grasp and glared down at him. "Did you not see what these miscreants just did? They must be punished!"

Aymer's gaze never wavered as he said, "Yes, they need to be punished, but he is just a boy! There is no need to strike him down. Aside from your wounded pride, the damage they have done is not so great. Besides," he looked around at all the men staring at the spectacle, "it may end up being talked about that the great Sir. Robert Clifford enjoys taking out his battlefield frustrations upon children."

That last comment filled Mr. Checkerboard with visible anger, but the sight of so many witnesses kept him in check. "Fine," he grumbled, "what do you suggest?"

Before Aymer could answer, the French guy spoke up, "If you'll permit me to interject, I have a few ideas."

This can't be good.

That French guy has a real mean streak, I thought as I lifted up a heavy wooden door and felt a splinter drive itself into my palm.

Contrary to what I had imagined; French guy, Mr. Checkerboard, and the rest of England's tin soldiers had not been spending their post-battle time sobbing in the fetal position. No, in reality they had been figuring out where to best position themselves tonight in order to make sure they would have the upper hand in the morning.

Not wanting anything separating them from their opponent, they made the decision to move their cavalry out of the woods of Torwood and onto the big open land of the battlefield. The only thing currently standing in their way was a long, winding river called the Bannock Burn. Though the river was technically passable (and a great source of water), they would still need several wooden boards to get their men and horses across the boggy ground.

Hence, our punishment. David, Winnie, and I were now being forced to help the soldiers pry off the doors and beams from local houses and barns and carry them over to the river.

"OW!" I screamed, dropping the heavy door on the ground. The splinter's sharp pain radiated through my hand.

"OY!" an English soldier yelled. He'd been holding the other end of the door when I'd dropped it, which caused him to also drop his end. "What'd ya do that for? You just about crushed my foot!"

"Well, it's not like it's my fault!" I yelled back at him, furious with the whole situation. "This stupid door is full of splinters! If you don't want me dropping it, how about providing some gloves or something?"

139

"Pick it up," came a growl from behind me. I didn't have to even turn around to know who'd said it, but I did. Yes, it was my dear friend, the French guy. He was really starting to work my last nerve.

"I need to see a medic. I have a splinter in my hand. Until I get it out, I don't know how you expect me to continuuuu . . ." All the wind was suddenly knocked out of my chest.

Frenchie's right fist was in my stomach and his left hand rested on my back. I felt his hot, sour breath when he leaned in towards my ear. "Did that hurt more than the splinter?"

I wheezed.

"Good. The next time that you want to stop working because of a little pain, just remember that I'm here to show you what real pain feels like. Do I make myself clear?"

Reluctantly, I mumbled, "Oui."

"Good," he said, releasing me from his grip. "Now pick up the door."

I looked over at the English guy on the other end who was now shifting his weight uncomfortably. I nodded, signaling to him that I was ready to lift. Together, we lifted the door into the air. Pain exploded through my arm and stomach, but I held steady. I just focused on moving one foot at a time as I made my way toward the river. Every so often, I'd start to lose my balance as my feet were sucked into the boggy earth. I was able to maintain my footing, but moving through the muck made every step twice as hard as it should have been.

By the time we'd reached the river I was sore, exhausted, and filthy. I looked up at the moon, wishing I was anywhere but here.

"Victor," said the Englishman who'd been helping lift, "let's go."

"To camp?" I asked hopefully.

He took a deep breath, clearly as exhausted as I was, "No, let's go get another one."

You've got to be kidding me!

Too tired to argue, I trudged behind him thinking, *I wonder what all the villagers will do when they come home from wherever they're hiding and discover that they no longer have doors? Hopefully they won't find deer and racoons sleeping in their beds.* Oh well, there was nothing I could do about it. All I could do was put one foot in front of the other.

For the rest of the night, we labored alongside the English army. Every once in a while, I'd see David or Winnie walk by, but was too tired to acknowledge the other's existence.

As the sun began to rise, the last of the English cavalry traversed across the muddy ground and across the Bannock Burn. David, Winnie, and I were taken back to camp and each tied to the base of a tree. For the first time since being there, I honestly didn't care about my captivity. All I cared about was sleep. Curling up in the dirt, I closed my eyes and listened to the birds sing their morning song. How the soldiers expected to battle after such a rough night, I really didn't know. But hey, that was their problem. As for my problems, they'd just have to wait 'til I woke up.

21

AVA

I was just about to leave the king's tent, when a loud commotion was heard outside. Hurrying to see what was the matter, King Robert and I raced outside. It was there that we found James Douglas and Robert Keith holding onto the arms of a bearded, blonde, and bedraggled looking man. His clothes were soaking wet and he was breathing heavily.

As soon as the stranger saw the king, he wrenched his arms away from Douglas and Keith's grasp and fell to his knees on the ground. "Your Majesty," he said, head bowed low, "have mercy on me. I do not come to harm, but to bring an important message to the true king of Scotland."

"This is Alexander Seton, Your Highness," Robert Keith said with a note of disdain in his voice. "He fights for Edward."

"Not anymore!" Alexander exclaimed, head briefly raising up in alarm before quickly dropping low once more. "I am sorry for my actions and wish to right my wrongs. I have been a coward. And though I understand if you should never want to see my face, I humbly ask that for Scotland's sake, you permit me to deliver a message."

I held my breath, anxiously awaiting this man's fate. I didn't have to wait long. Robert strode over to the man, standing in front of him like a towering tree, then extended his right hand. The man cautiously looked up, first at the hand, then into King Robert's face. Somewhat stunned, he grabbed ahold of the hand and allowed himself to be pulled up onto his feet.

"Alexander," Robert began, "all acts you have committed against Scotland have been pardoned, and it fills me with great pleasure to welcome back one of our own." Alexander's lip quivered, and he was about to drop back to the floor, when Robert grabbed hold of his shoulders with a laugh and said, "But I do not intend to hear your message if you wallow on the ground!"

Relieved, Alexander smiled.

"What is it that you've traveled here to tell me?"

Alexander spoke with a sense of urgency. "The English are weak. Do not be fooled by their numbers. They are an army formed against their will, pushed to their physical limits, and unconvinced of their own righteousness. They are a house built on crumbling sand. Now is the time to tear them down."

"I see," King Robert said, pondering what he'd just heard.

With annoyance, Keith pointed a finger at Alexander, "How can we trust this man? For all we know, he could be a spy!"

Alexander was about to speak up when King Robert interjected, "Do you trust me?"

"Of . . . of course," Keith stammered.

"Then trust me when I say that I have looked into this man's eyes and have found no deception." Keith's mouth clamped shut. "It is because of this that I am confident in my decision to face off against the English tomorrow."

Keith looked a bit nervous, but ultimately said, "Than I shall fight with you 'til the end."

"Your Highness!" shouted a young boy, not much older than 18, who was making his way toward our group with a couple of other men. "We've received word from our scouts keeping watch over the English army. They're making moves to cross the Bannock Burn tonight."

"Are they staying south of the Pelstream Burn?" Robert asked.

"Yes, they are."

The king nodded. "Then I know what we're going to do. Tomorrow, our men will form their schiltron formations. Maintaining those formations, we are going to march forward and meet the enemy on their side of the battlefield."

"Are you sure?" James Douglas asked. "I mean, do you think our men are ready? I know we've been practicing a moveable schiltron formation, but those have only been drills. Never before have foot soldiers moved forward to meet the might of knights on horseback."

"Our men have already proved their worth on the battlefield today," the king replied. "Besides, the English are showing through their movements that they expect us to just sit and wait for their attack. If they didn't, they would not be currently situating themselves on a piece of land that is hemmed in on three sides by rivers. Better yet, what our visiting friends most likely do not realize is that the Bannock Burn and Pelstream Burn are both tidal rivers. Mark my words, the waters will very soon rise to levels that will be impassable."

"We'll block them in," James said, brightening at the sudden realization, "and they won't have anywhere to run."

"That's right, James," King Robert said, looking around at the men before him. "Tomorrow I am trusting you all to help lead Scotland's army with confidence because we have 'right' on our side. Domination is the only desire that drives our enemies. But what is it that we fight for? We fight for our lives. We fight for our families. We fight for the freedom of our country!

"You aren't with me now because you long to live a life of timidity. If that were so, you could have lived quietly as slaves. No, what you desire is freedom. And so tomorrow, I ask and pray that you advance upon the enemy with such boldness that you cause even the men in the back to tremble! I pray that tomorrow you find yourselves valiant, strong and undismayed." He sighed. "You know what honor is. Now is the time to fight with honor."

Every eye was fixated on King Robert. So much so that I doubted much attention was paid to me as I backed away from the group and slipped out of sight. I knew that King Robert hadn't been speaking to me, yet somehow, he had been. The time had come for me to also be valiant, strong, and undismayed.

As soon as I'd entered our tent (which had been put together several hours earlier), a frizzy ball of orange hair leapt at me.

"Ava, you're back!" Cassidy screamed. "I was getting worried! Nolan told me what he'd said and what you'd said and how you'd walked off into the woods at night all by yourself. I was going to go look for you, but I didn't know where you'd gone and my sense of direction isn't terribly reliable. I mean, I could have risked it and gone out anyway, but what if you'd come back and then I was lost in the woods. Would that be better? Am I being selfish?"

"No, it wouldn't and no, you're not," I said, putting a stop to the verbal runaway train. "You did the right thing. I'm back. Everything's okay."

"Is it?" came Nolan's voice. He was sitting in the corner of the tent with the metal ball in his lap.

I took a deep breath, our last argument flashing through my mind. "Yeah, Nolan, it is."

"For the record, I didn't . . ."

"Nolan," I said, firmly, "everything's okay."

A look was shared between us that spoke more than any words could have. After the conversation I'd had with King Robert, I realized that I needed to move on. I needed to move on from my past, my pain, my guilt, and my resentment. I was determined to allow this moment to be a fresh start. Not just for myself, but for everyone.

"So," I said, pointing to the metal ball, "did you figure that thing out yet?"

"Yeah right," Nolan scoffed, obviously frustrated, "right now its sole purpose is to taunt me."

"Well, if I were you, I'd pack it back up and get a good night's sleep. We're leaving tomorrow."

"Where are we going?" Cassidy asked.

Feeling newfound determination coursing through my veins, I said, "We're going to get our friends."

After a restless night, I awoke bright and early on the 24th of June, the feast day of St. John the Baptist. To Nolan's delight, the Saint's feast day was celebrated with a nice assortment of food including meat, fruit, and vegetables. "Now this is what I call a celebration!" he said with delight, as he took a big bite out of a sandwich he'd constructed. It wasn't the type of abundance you'd expect at Thanksgiving, but it was most certainly better than the selection we'd had yesterday.

After we'd finished eating breakfast; Nolan, Cassidy, and I helped Agnes pass out food to the soldiers who were already in position on the battlefield. We went from group to group, following the priests who were giving an on-location mass. The soldiers were so moved by the words of scripture, that I found many of them still deep in prayer when I had to awkwardly ask, "Cheese?"

Never before had I seen a church service impact so many, so deeply. Then again, who was to say that it wouldn't be the last one they'd ever hear?

Trying to push that depressing thought away, I turned my attention to the sun's rays bouncing off the gleaming silver of the English army. *Bad idea. Not helping.*

Luckily, before anxiety could completely overwhelm me, King Robert rode over and provided me with a distraction. One-by-one he called out several soldiers and had them kneel before him. Unsheathing his sword, he knighted each one before their fellow countrymen.

I couldn't help but smile as I saw James Douglas move forward to receive this special honor. Just a couple days ago, I'd thought of him as a creepy vampire in the woods. Now, I was seeing him in a whole new light. "You go, James," I murmured.

And though I could have been imagining things, I thought I saw the corners of King Robert's lips turn up a little bit higher as he raised his blade and knighted his loyal friend.

When the ceremony was finished, King Robert mounted his horse and bellowed into the air, "The time has come to advance! But before we reach the enemy, I'll signal you all to kneel. It is at that time that we will submit ourselves to the true king of Scotland and of all the Earth, our Lord and Savior Jesus Christ! Our fate is in His hands, and it is His will that shall be done." Grabbing the reigns of his horse, he spun around to face what lie ahead. The golden banner of Scotland with its single red lion swayed in the breeze. Then raising his blade to the sky, he beckoned, "ONWARD!"

Spears in hand, men who were once farmers, carpenters, noblemen, and millers walked side-by-side and became soldiers. As I watched them go, I lifted up a quick prayer to the Lord, *God, please watch over them and protect them. And please be with their families. Amen.*

"Ava," Agnes called out to me, "lessen you want to spear the English yourself, I suggest we make our way back."

"Right, coming!" I pretended to obediently follow Agnes back to camp, but darted behind a tree when she wasn't looking. Nolan and Cassidy did the same. This was because last night, I'd realized that there would be no better time to free our friends than when the battle was raging.

22

DAVID

"I CAN'T SWIM!" I screamed, drowning in both panic and water. The river's gushing torrent pushed my head below the churning surface and into its echoey chamber of suffocating darkness. Searing pain ran through my fingers as they desperately clenched around a wood beam that was my only lifeline. *Don't let go!*

Lifesaving oxygen filled my lungs as I bobbed back up to the surface and gasped for air. I heard Winnie scream, "DAVID!" just before my ears were once again filled with the water I was sure was about to kill me.

That morning had begun like any other morning in Scotland. I'd opened my eyes to a bright and sunny day, yawned, tried to stretch, and then remembered I was tied to something. Yep, good old Scotland!

But things had started looking up when Winnie's cute face popped up in front of mine with a cheery, "Good morning!"

"Winnie!" I said with alarm. "What are you doing here? Why aren't you tied up?"

She flashed a smile as she held up a small knife and began to cut my ropes. Apparently, there were some advantages to being a person others often overlooked. During our punishment of building pathways to cross the river, she'd taken a page out of Victor's playbook and incited a verbal argument between two men who had strong opinions about whether Gilbert de Claire or Humphry de Bohun should be leading the army. They hadn't noticed when she'd slipped one of their blades out of its sheath and tucked it underneath her Providence blazer.

"Winnie, you're my hero!" I said, as the last of my bondages fell to the ground. She blushed.

A few minutes later, all three of us were running as fast as we could toward the river. We may not have known where Cassidy, Nolan, and Ava were; but we knew where Alexander Seton was. He was at the Scottish camp. If he could put in a good word for us, then maybe, just maybe, there would be people who could help us find our friends and get us out of here.

"What happened?" Victor asked, staring at the Bannock Burn. What had once been a flowing stream, had become a raging river that snaked through the trees, ready to devour its prey.

My heart sank. "It got bigger."

"Great, that's just great!" Victor yelled, picking up and hurling a stone into the water. It landed with a *thunk*.

Thunk? That didn't seem right. Winnie walked closer to the river and pointed into the water, "Look!"

There it was, below the surface of the water was a long, wooden beam that spanned the length of the river. It maintained its position, stuck between a series of large boulders.

It was a miracle! We were in need of a way to cross the river, and as if placed by the hands of God Himself, a tightrope-like exit strategy was placed before us. Considering this, was it any wonder I yelled out, "No freakin' way!" in a voice that showcased my complete horror?

Okay, maybe not the reaction you'd expect. But come on! That beam wasn't even wide enough to put two feet side by side. Plus, what guarantee did we even have that it would remain in place once we put our weight on it? The rocks and the waves were battling each other for supremacy, and my money was on the waves!

"Come on, David," Victor said, "it's our only chance!"

"At what? Drowning?"

150

"We can't stay here."

"Says who? It's a theory. I say we test it out. All in favor?" I shot my arm high into the air, hoping to see Winnie's go up too. She just stood there.

"Well, I don't plan on waiting around to be captured again! Stay here if you want, but I'm crossing this river with or without you!" With that, Victor took the first step into the water. I held my breath, watching him inch his way across the beam. He kept himself low, one foot in front of the other, hands holding onto the beam. Slowly but surely, he crept across like a cat all the way to the other side.

Relieved to see he'd made it, I finally felt myself exhale.

"COME ON, WINNIE," he yelled from across the river.

She looked over at me and nervously bit her lip. Her hands shook as she submerged them into the water and grasped the beam. Inch by inch, she made her way across. A couple of times she wobbled, making my heart skip a beat, but she managed to recover her footing.

Both safely across, Winnie and Victor looked over at me expectantly. *Water, why did it have to be water?* When I was 5, my older brother had tried teaching me to swim by throwing me into the deep end of our family pool. My dad dove in and pulled me out, but I had hated water ever since.

"DAVID! COME ON!" Victor screamed.

It was now or never. *You can do this,* I told myself, *Victor and Winnie made it across. You can, too.* The water was colder than I'd expected, increasing my desire to retreat, but I didn't. I focused my eyes on the (somewhat) solid foundation below me and cautiously began to move.

It wasn't easy, but I was making it work. That is, until I lost focus. Halfway across, I made the mistake of looking not at the beam, but at the thunderous waves rushing toward me. In the blink of an eye, my foot slipped, sending my whole body into the chilly water.

Acting fast, I wrapped my hands around the beam and held on tight. Bobbing in and out of the water, every breath I took became a choking mixture of water and oxygen. Still, I managed to cry out, "I CAN'T SWIM!" before being dunked once again into my worst nightmare.

I knew I couldn't hold on much longer. Victor had been right, I had butterfingers. And those butterfingers were losing their grasp on my last strand of hope.

But as soon as my hands gave way to their fate, I felt a hand grasp around my wrist. Eyes breaking through the surface of the water, I came face-to-face with Victor. His whole body was sprawled along the beam and he was holding onto me with all his might.

"GRAB AHOLD OF MY HAND!" he commanded. Twisting my hand around, I locked my fingers around his wrist. With a mighty tug, he pulled me back to the beam. Back to safety. Lifting myself across it, I took a moment to regain my breath.

"Can you move?" Victor asked.

I nodded.

Together, we crawled to shore on our bellies before collapsing in the dirt. I loved dirt. I loved grass. I loved solid land!

"David?" Victor asked, sprawled out next to me.

I looked over at him, "Yeah?"

"When were you going to tell me you couldn't swim?"

I laughed, choking up the last of the water in my lungs. There had been times in our friendship when I'd wondered if Victor cared whether I lived or died. Now I knew.

When I think of great war movies, I think of men crawling across the ground on their bellies. Yes, it's a classic. Explosions erupting above their heads, war paint streaked across their faces, those brave army men crawled their way to freedom.

This was the image I thought about as I bellied up to the earth and wiggled as close as I dared get behind the English army. I was now one of those brave men.

Ow. The ground was really hard. *Ow!* A rock went into the soft part of my knee. *OWWW!* I got stabbed by a twig! *These crawling sequences look so much cooler in the movies.*

I ducked low behind a bush. Winnie and Victor did the same. Originally, we'd planned on going around the perimeter of the battlefield and avoiding the English army all together. Unfortunately for us, they were spread out in such a way that trapped us between them and the river.

With no chance on earth of me going back across that river, we decided to sneak up behind them, wait until they marched across the field, and then run like the wind. Once they moved forward, they would hopefully open up a space for us to slip around the scary battle stuff and get to the Scottish camp safely.

Now only a few feet away from the last row of soldiers, I could hear some of them talking. "That's the strangest thing I've ever seen," one of them said, "The Scotsmen are coming to meet us on foot!"

"No they're not," said another, "look, they're kneeling on the ground, begging us for mercy."

The first one grunted, "Begging for mercy, yes, but not from us. How is it you've forgotten what it looks like to pray?"

Before the second one could reply, trumpet blasts sounded through the air. The battle had officially begun.

23

AVA

From behind my selected tree, I watched as the Scottish army pressed in shoulder-to-shoulder and raised their spears. Almost immediately, a trumpet sounded, followed by a stampede of English horses. One knight was so eager to fight, that he dashed off ahead of everyone else with his outer yellow garment still in the hands of the young boy who had been trying to secure it to him.

For all his passion, though, he failed to achieve glory as his horse was quickly met with the sharpened end of the Scottish spears. Thrown off the steed, his fate was sealed.

That knight was only the first of many who found themselves dismounted and defeated, reduced to feeling the full weight of their armor. As the battle intensified, the sickening sound of screams mixed with the clanking of metal-on-metal. What once was a beautiful morning was now filled with darkness.

I wanted to look away, but knew I couldn't. If we were going to cross the battlefield, we had to make sure our timing was perfect. The plan was to wait until the Scottish army had completely hemmed in the English between the Bannock and Pelstream rivers. Once the English were contained, we'd make our way around the fighting and over to the English camp.

"Ava!" Cassidy called. "Which way are we going to be running?"

"What?" I asked.

"Which way are we running? North or south?"

Oh no, I hadn't figured that part out! It had seemed like such a simple solution at the time: run around. *How could I have been so stupid?* It was just like me to start doing something before I'd fully thought it out.

"I say we go south and follow the road," Nolan said.

Cassidy clearly disagreed. "Ah yes, and I'm sure the English would have been careless enough to leave it open for just anyone to escape. Think Nolan!"

"I am thinking! I'm thinking that we have no idea what the terrain is like to the north. Will we even be able to get around? At least we know the road goes that direction!"

"Yeah, us and everybody else!"

"Stop it!" I yelled, silencing their bickering. I had to think. It was true that the south did look the best, but it was an obvious exit strategy that would put us completely out in the open. The north looked clear if we looped around the outside of the rivers, but Nolan was right, we had no way of knowing if the area was passable.

"Which way?" Cassidy asked.

Both she and Nolan were looking at me, waiting for some words of wisdom I didn't have. I had to make a choice. Desperate for some guidance, I closed my eyes and lifted up a prayer. *God, I don't know what to do. Please help us!*

I opened my eyes. The Scottish schiltrons were on the move, pressing the English into their watery cage. I was running out of time. I looked at each of my options and knew what we had to do. They didn't look any different. There wasn't a giant arrow blazing through the sky, showing me which way to go. All I had was a feeling, barely more than a whisper. A feeling that anyone but me would have explained away as just a gut instinct originating from inside myself. But I knew different. I knew that a moment ago, all I had felt was confusion and panic. Now, I felt sure and calm. "We're running north."

"We don't know what's over there!" Nolan protested.

"I know," I said, looking into his eyes, "but can you trust me?"

He paused for a moment, struggling to commit. "Okay," he relented, then smiled. "I'm willing to follow the Ice Queen into battle."

I had to laugh. Despite all the times Nolan had annoyed me or made me angry, I couldn't help but like the guy. Filled with a mischievous spirit, I replied, "Oh come on, Nolan, we both know that's not true. According to you, everybody at school knows . . . I'm really the Outlaw Queen."

He chuckled as soon as he realized that I wasn't mad or offended, just having fun. "Alright Outlaw Queen, when do we run?"

I looked out. James Douglas had closed the gap between the Pelstream Burn and the other Scotsmen. The English were trapped. With a surge of adrenaline coursing through my veins, I shouted, "NOW!"

24

WINNIE

If it were possible to get what you wanted just by wishing it with all your might, I would have been home a long time ago. Crouched low, hiding within the sharp embrace of a bush, I squeezed my eyes shut and covered my ears with my hands. The violence erupting behind me was too much to bear. But try as I might, the sound of screams and frenzied shouting still managed to slip through my fingers.

The pounding of the earth made my eyes fly open just moments before an injured horse burst through a nearby bush, missing me by only a couple of feet. It was a close call, and my heart was still pounding as a hand wrapped around my wrist. "AHHHHH!" I screamed.

"Winnie, it's me!" David said, pulling one of my hands away from my ear. "We have to go. The army isn't moving forward. It's being pressed backward. Pretty soon, it won't be safe here."

Just then, as if emphasizing his point, another runaway horse burst through the foliage behind him, dragging along a soldier who was caught in its reigns. Fear welled up within me and transformed into tears. "Where are we going to go?" I choked out. "There's nowhere to go!"

"Victor heard the archers yelling at each other to head north and try to cross the Pelstream Burn. It might be shallower up there."

I just stared at him. David's voice had been only one amongst a thousand more that were overloading my senses.

"Winnie?" he asked with a look of concern. "We have to go *now*. We might not get another chance. Do you understand?"

I pressed my eyes together, squeezing out one last tear before nodding reluctantly. I felt David grab my hand and allowed him to pull me out from my hiding place and into the open. We ran toward Victor and kept on going, stopping only to dodge the occasional piece of battle debris. The only good thing about the fighting was that the English were far too preoccupied with the Scots to have any concern for the three of us.

"LOOK!" Victor shouted, pointing up ahead and to the left. "The archers must have crossed the river." Indeed, a hail of arrows was pouring down like bitter rain upon the Scottish army. The spearmen closest to the northern end fell one by one, disappearing beneath the surface of the crowd. The sight made my legs stiffen up, but David kept pulling me along.

"We're almost there!" David yelled, pointing to the bend in the river. The closer we got, the clearer it became that the Pelstream Burn did actually narrow. A slight glimmer of hope warmed my heart. We might be able to get out of there.

However, that hope was snuffed out the instant we reached the water and saw hundreds of English archers skidding down the hillside and splashing back across the Pelstream.

"Why are they coming back?" Victor asked.

His question was answered when we looked up the hillside and saw the glint of steel, followed by the body of an English archer tumbling down the hill. The Scots had raced to meet their foes and put an end to the aerial attacks. Unbeknownst to them, though, they had also put an end to our escape plan.

25

AVA

Running across the battlefield wasn't like running on the track at school. The ground sloped in surprising areas and grass hid divots that tripped us up on more than one occasion.

Our pace felt incredibly slow when compared to Robert Keith's squadron of horsemen that barreled past us, heading straight toward a group of English archers who were decimating James Douglas' men.

"OW!" I heard Cassidy scream, causing me to turn around. She'd tripped and was lying with her face in the dirt.

"Are you okay?" I asked, running over to help her up.

"Yeah, I'm . . . OW!" She dropped a little, but Nolan and I held her up.

"What is it?" Nolan asked.

"It's my ankle," she said. "I tripped in a hole and must have twisted it."

"Can you put any weight on it at all?" I asked.

She gingerly set her foot down and tried to stand, but must have immediately regretted it. She winced and bit her lip, shaking her head in response.

"Here," Nolan said, sliding the jacket-backpack containing the ball off his shoulders and handing it to me. He then squatted down and said to Cassidy, "Get on."

"You can't carry me all that way," she protested.

"Of course I can. God made you small and portable. Hop on and let's get going!" Cassidy wrapped her arms around his neck and was hoisted into the air. "Guess you can't laugh anymore about me falling into a hole."

"Why not?" she asked. "Yours was a pit, remember? There's a difference."

"I can drop you," he quipped.

"Guys," I said impatiently, "let's move it!"

We made our way around the outer edge of the Pelstream Burn, giving a wide berth so as to avoid the fighting. It made our route longer, but safer.

The barrage of arrows that had been assaulting the Scots became thinner and thinner until they stopped altogether. Robert Keith's team had done their job.

I looked back a couple of times at Nolan. He was breathing heavier, and his gaze was hardened, but he never complained about the extra weight on his back.

As we rounded the Pelstream's outer edges, trees and bushes popped up sporadically, quenching their thirst with the river's water. If I looked between them, I could see English soldiers being pushed back deeper and deeper into their limited piece of land.

Nolan stopped as soon as we hit a thick blanket of trees that adorned a hillside. Looking up at the top of it, he said, "I think we should take a break." Cassidy slid off his back and the two collapsed on the ground, facing the path we'd just traversed. I ignored my impatient heart and joined them.

Sweat dripped in ribbons down my forehead and Cassidy looked like she was getting a sunburn. The sound of the river on my left reminded me how thirsty I was.

"Look," Cassidy said, pointing to a commotion down river. Englishmen on horseback were breaking through the Scottish barricades and attempting to flee across the river. The Scots tried to restrain their flight, but were knocked to the ground by a knight wielding an iron mace. Still, they managed to capture one who was holding a shield with three elongated lions on it. As the Scottish soldiers pulled him off his horse, I watched as those three golden lions were pulled back into the frenzy and consumed.

162

The three knights who broke their way free, rode as fast as they could toward Stirling Castle.

"Did you see what that one knight was wearing?" Cassidy asked.

"Yeah," I said, "which means he wasn't a knight. He was the king."

A thick breeze swirled around me. It was the kind of breeze that let you know a storm was brewing.

26

VICTOR

I was in a bush. Again. *Think, Victor, think! There has to be a way out of here.* The English had been pushed so far back, that there was no way we could just go back the way we came. And unless we acquired some weaponry, there was a better than average chance the Scottish troops would make short work of us if we tried to cross the river. We were stuck between a rock and a hard place. Or in this case, between a river and a prickly place.

Just then, the entire atmosphere changed. The earth shook with the sounds of soldiers and mounted knights on horseback racing past us, desperate to cross the Pelstream and Bannock rivers. Never would I need to wonder what it would be like to be caught in the middle of a stampede. Curling myself up as small as possible, I prayed I wouldn't get trampled.

A few moments later, I felt the *thud* of another person ramming into my shoulder. I looked over to see a wrinkled old man with a whitening dark-red beard squeezing in next to me. "Hey!" I shouted. "Get your own bush!"

He ignored my protest, removed a metal shin guard, and tossed it into the fray. "Forgot that one," he said and extended his hand. Stunned, I shook it out of sheer habit. He whispered, "I'm Sir. Marmaduke Tweng. Looks like we had the same idea."

"Yeah," I said, "and I was here first."

"And I was here second. Good to know you've learned to count! Now, unless you are keener than I at the thought of being trampled or drowning, I suggest you hush up and pretend you're foliage." With that, the odd little man squished up next to me and said not another word. Awkward.

27

AVA

"I told you we should have gone south," Nolan grumbled. We'd climbed up the hill, only to find ourselves blocked by the flowing monstrosity that fed the Pelstream and Bannock rivers.

"There has to be a way across," I said, trying to convince myself as much as Nolan.

He crossed his arms, "Where?"

I looked in both directions. It didn't make sense. I'd felt so sure that this was the way we needed to go. I'd thought God was helping us, guiding us. But now?

I heard screaming coming from downstream. I walked toward the edge of the hill and looked out over the treetops down onto the battlefield. The English were retreating, trying to escape in every direction. Multitudes ran toward the Bannock Burn, but I didn't see many come out on the other side.

It was too late. I knew any soldiers who successfully made it out would head straight back to camp, reaching it long before the three of us could figure out how to get across the river.

Nolan helped Cassidy hobble over next to me. "What do we do now?" she asked.

With a sigh, I admitted, "I don't know." Before, I'd felt sure. Guided. Was I wrong? A moment ago, I'd convinced Nolan and Cassidy to follow me. Ugh, I felt sick.

"I didn't know Bruce had reserved that many soldiers," Nolan said, pointing off in the distance. I followed his gaze and saw hundreds of people running across the field from the Scottish camp. They were shouting and waving weapons. In response, a greater number of English soldiers joined the mass exodus.

"He didn't," I said, a bit of amusement breaking through my heavy heart. "Look again."

The closer they got, the clearer it became that the terrifying mass of Scottish reinforcements was not a well-trained or well-outfitted militia— simply a very large and very angry group of camp followers.

"Is that . . ." Cassidy squinted, "Agnes?"

Sure enough, pulling up the rear, was the formidable woman I'd come to love and fear. Scooting along, as fast as her feet could shuffle, wielding a pitchfork in one hand. "Yep," I said, "that's our Agnes." For a moment, I wondered if I should lift up a prayer for protection—for the English, that is!

As happy as I was that Bruce and his men were winning (an outcome I never would have predicted a day or two ago) the thought of losing our friends for good clouded over everything else.

"A storm's coming," Nolan noted, looking out beyond the Scottish camp at the grey skies rolling in.

"Figures," I mumbled. My eyes scanned over the broken remains of the battlefield, trying not to focus too long on the carnage strewn across the ground. Small groupings of determined soldiers remained fighting, their numbers dwindling. It was like watching a fire slowly burn out.

As my eyes roved lower, nearing the ground that surrounded the fork in the rivers, I couldn't believe what I was seeing. There, crouched behind an assortment of bushes, was Winnie, David, Victor, and a random old guy invading Victor's personal space.

"IT'S THEM! IT'S THEM!" I shouted, feeling as if my heart was exploding in my chest.

"What? Who?" Cassidy asked.

"Our friends! They're right there!"

"Where?" asked Nolan.

"Right there, behind those bushes. Don't you see?" A moment later, they did. Confusion turned to joy and the three of us were leaping in the air and waving our arms, trying to get their attention. Well, Cassidy didn't exactly leap, but the sentiment was there. I was just so happy; I couldn't believe it! North really was the right way to go.

"They don't see us," Nolan panted, his voice laced with growing concern.

"Then let's go get them," Cassidy said.

"How?" he asked. "The river is standing in our way. If we go down to the water's edge, the trees will block their view of us."

"We can go back the way we came. Once the battle is over, we can go to them."

"But they don't even know we're looking for them! What if they leave and head in another direction? Or worse, are captured again?" Silence.

He was right. We needed to show them where we were, and that we were looking for them. More importantly, we needed to get them to safety. "Let's try something else," I said, grabbing the ball. I unwrapped it and discarded it on the ground. Tying the jackets to a nearby stick, I waved my makeshift flag in the air until my burning arms cried out for a break. Nothing.

"What now?" Nolan asked. Once again, I didn't know. It was like every time we solved one problem, another reared its ugly head. Why couldn't anything be simple?

I bent down and picked up the metal ball that was lying on the ground. Frustration pulsed through my hands. I wanted to throw that stupid thing so bad! I stared into its reflective surface, my hands shaking with anger. Suddenly, I saw blue. A pulse of blue light had appeared for a split second, then disappeared. Startled, I screamed and dropped the ball.

"What's the matter?" Cassidy asked.

I pointed at it.

Nolan looked at the motionless object, unimpressed. "What?"

"I saw blue," I said. "It was there for just a split second, but it was there."

Cassidy looked scared, "What did you do?"

"I . . . I don't know!" Just then, out of the corner of my eye, I saw a streak of white light race down the distant, darkening sky. A split second later, the ball flickered blue. Its glow lasted slightly longer than the first time, but ebbed out.

"STOP IT!" Cassidy screamed.

"I didn't do it," I protested. "It . . . it . . ." I stopped talking. The puzzle pieces quickly fit inside my head, forming a beautiful picture I didn't know I'd been trying to create. "It's the lightning," I breathed.

Cassidy scrunched up her face, "What?"

"It's the lightning!" I started pacing back and forth, unable to contain the excitement. "Don't you see? The day we left Providence, there was a storm and lightning. When we went down the hole, I heard the sound of a train. Cassidy, that ghost story at school, when did the students hear the sound of the train?"

"Uh . . ." she hesitated, startled by my unusual demeanor, "during storms."

"During storms, that's right! Now look out there, what do you see?"

Nolan and Cassidy turned.

"There's a storm," Nolan said slowly.

"Exactly!" I stopped pacing and took a moment to regain control of my breath. "The lightning is it's 'on' switch."

"But why did it only glow a little bit?" Nolan asked.

"Because," Cassidy said, quickly catching up, "it's far away."

"Exactly!" I said. "And I'm willing to bet that the closer that storm gets, the longer our blue ball will stay charged."

"And we'll be sent home," Nolan said.

Cassidy's face fell, "Without our friends."

The statement hit us hard. For a brief moment, we looked at each other. Then, as if a starter's pistol was shot into the air, the race was on!

"Start getting Cassidy down the hill," I barked at Nolan. "I'll grab the ball!" He wrapped his arm underneath hers and started to half-carry half-drag her down the hill toward the river.

I lunged for the ball, but tripped backward when a bolt of lightning triggered an even brighter flash of blue light that startled me. It held on for a few seconds, pulsed a couple of times, and went dark. Wide eyed, I quickly looked out at our friends in the field. My eyes locked with David's. We stared at each other a moment, stunned. I pointed at the river. He nodded.

28

DAVID

"Don't try to cross the river!" I heard the old man warn as I grabbed Victor's hand and pulled him to his feet. I kept ahold of him with my left hand and Winnie with my right as I pulled both of them away from our security shrubs.

"What are you doing?" Victor asked.

"We have to go!" I yelled, and steered them toward the place where the Bannock Burn forks, dividing the land into three separate sections. Victor resisted, violently yanking his arm away.

"Are you mad?" he screamed. "There's a reason nobody's trying to cross at that section. We were safer where we were!"

"I saw it!" I yelled back.

"Saw what?"

"The others. The blue light. They were up on that hill!"

"The blue light? Are you sure?" he asked, realization dawning on him.

"Yes! Now, let's go!" No further discussion was needed as we ran the rest of the way there.

Skidding to a stop at the river's edge, we didn't have to wait long before we saw Nolan and Cassidy ungracefully careening down the slope on the other side. It was shocking to see them in period-appropriate clothing, but

I was more concerned with the fact that Cassidy looked hurt. She was leaning on Nolan for support, and every once in a while, her face would twist itself in pain.

"CASSIDY!" Winnie screamed, something I hadn't been aware she could even do.

Seeing Winnie again must have overridden Cassidy's pain, because as soon as she heard her friend's voice, she looked up with a huge smile on her face.

"NOLAN," Victor called out, "WHERE'S AVA? WHERE'S THE BALL?"

Before Nolan could answer, Ava bounded down the hillside. She was holding onto the metal ball, dodging trees and brush. Lightning struck in the distance. Just then, the metal orb burst with blinding blue light. The power of it caused Ava to let go, sending it rolling down the hill. It turned itself off as it neared the water's edge, but didn't stop its trajectory. From that point on, it felt like I was watching everything happen in slow motion. The metal ball, our only hope of escape, tumbled straight into the water with a gut-wrenching *splash*.

"NOOOO!" Victor cried and ran over to the turbulent waters, unable to do anything to change the outcome.

As the rest of us slowly made our way over, Ava looked at me with an expression that couldn't have meant anything other than, "I'm sorry."

But just when I thought all hope was lost, I heard a loud *crack* explode from the sky. The river's water radiated an abnormally blue glow, spinning faster and faster like a liquid tornado. Out of the center, the ball sprung into the air and hovered in place, with both its halves turning at the same speed as the water. The last time this had happened, the vortex had sucked me in. This time, I jumped.

29

AVA

For a moment, I didn't know where I was. It all felt like I was waking from a dream, but while the gentle patter of raindrops on a window pane urged me to go back to sleep, the cold sting of the cement floor I was lying on convinced me to get up. Blinking the haze away, the new morning light coming in from a dirty basement window showed me that I was back in Dr. Keller's laboratory. Beakers and microscopes were smashed on the floor, accompanied by the occasional large river rock. Nolan, Cassidy, Winnie, David, and Victor were all there; still wearing their dirty, if not downright unusual, clothing. No, it hadn't been a dream.

Few words were spoken as we picked ourselves up and tried to recover from the shock of it all. At some point, it was David who broke the silence with, "Well . . . that was different." The laughter that followed was warm and healing. We were back. We were home.

Winnie shuffled over to a corner of the room, bent down, and picked something up off the floor.

"What's that?" Cassidy asked.

Winnie turned around and held up a book. "I borrowed this from Dr. Keller's office. At the time, I'd thought he'd written down random stories from history. It seemed odd. But now I'm wondering, what if he wasn't writing down the past, but his present? His adventures."

I walked over to Winnie and she handed me the book. I ran my hand over the gold lettering, wiping off bits of debris as I read, *"The Lightning Sphere Reports."* It was the second time I'd heard those words, but it felt like the first. It all made sense now.

Nolan picked up the metal ball from off the ground. "So," he said, "looks like we found the lightning sphere."

"What do we do with it?" Victor asked. We all exchanged nervous looks.

"We should put it back," Cassidy said. "It's too dangerous."

"Yeah," David agreed, "we should put it back."

Nobody protested as we placed the lightning sphere back into its metal box. But as I watched the lid lower, obscuring it from view, I had the strangest feeling that someday, I'd see it again.

Since Maci had moved all my clothes to the basement, Cassidy and I were able to change out of our medieval dresses before going upstairs and encountering the modern world. Nolan, on the other hand, opted to wait in the basement until David could bring him back a fresh uniform.

Even though everyone was tired, and Cassidy had a hurt ankle, they still offered to help me get my stuff back to the dorm. Winnie and Cassidy removed my clothes from the metal ceiling wires, while the boys took on the heavy lifting. I felt grateful that I had finally found good friends.

"Beep, beep, coming through!" Victor said to Maci, making her squeeze against the wall as they wedged my bed through the doorway of my dorm room.

"Oh good, she's back," Maci mumbled half-heartedly. Needing to get my desk, the boys left, giving me a few awkward minutes alone with my roommate. "Didn't you like your new room?" she asked, her tone dripping with venom.

A thousand hurtful words hammered at my lips, wanting to be let out, to hurt her as deeply as she hurt me. But they were held at bay when I remembered what King Robert had said to me . . .

"I think you'll find that when you start focusing on pleasing the True King with your actions, that there will be others who eventually see you for who you really are."

The True King, I thought as my hand reached for my necklace, fingers tightening around the little cross my mother had given me.

"Maci . . ." I said slowly, not completely wanting to say what I was about to, "I know you think I'm a criminal. . . . Because I was. But I didn't steal your necklace." She opened her mouth to speak, but I barreled on, not wanting her to make things harder for me. "I know you may not believe me, but it's the truth!" I couldn't stop my hands from shaking a little as I unhooked the cross necklace from around my neck. "Now, I know this isn't as expensive as the one you lost, but it's the only piece of jewelry I own. If you'd like it, you can have it."

I'm not sure how to describe the feeling I had as I placed my treasured object into her palm. But as soon as I let go, I felt at peace. I didn't know what Maci would do with my necklace, and in a way, I didn't care. I knew that I had done the right thing by trying to make peace. Besides, deep down I knew that when my mother had given me that necklace, she'd been trying to give me a gift far more valuable than jewelry.

Maci looked down at it, her features briefly softening. Then she cleared her throat and held out the necklace, resuming her prideful demeanor. "Take it, I don't wear cheap junk." As soon as I regained possession of it, she spun around and sat in her desk chair. "Besides," she said, "I found my necklace."

"You did?" I asked. "Where was it?"

"Apparently, when the school staff came to drop off your bags, they bumped my nightstand which caused the necklace to fall behind it. If I hadn't needed to plug in my curling iron this morning, I never would have found it." She flicked her hand up, examining her cuticles. "I'll have to make the school aware of their incompetence."

"Okay . . ." I said, "so we're cool?"

She looked up from her nails and paused. Then she got up, grabbed her backpack off the ground, slung it over her shoulder, and walked over to me. I expected her to say something. Instead, she reached into her jacket pocket and pulled out a clicker. With a press of the button, I heard the *beep*, that indicated a set alarm on her closet. Then she flashed a condescending smile and walked out the door.

For the next couple of days, it seemed like everything reminded me of Scotland. When I put on my school uniform, I remembered the strange looks we'd all gotten because of them. When the school's cafeteria lady served us our food, I thought of Agnes and how she took such pride in her cooking. And when I went to sleep at night, I closed my eyes and imagined the stars that had blanketed the night sky.

I felt the experience had changed me in some ways, and I wasn't the only one. The differences in the others were subtle, but definitely there. The boys were no longer trying to aggravate us every five minutes, Winnie found the courage to eat in the cafeteria (even when some of the kids snickered at her), and Cassidy . . .

"Can I come in?" I asked, opening up the door to Cassidy and Winnie's room. Cassidy was sitting on her bed with her wrapped ankle propped up on a pillow.

"Of course," she said, grabbing her homework and tossing it off the foot of the bed so I could have a seat.

"How's your ankle?"

"Much better. Honestly, though, I'm enjoying sitting out of gym class."

"Why?" I asked with feigned confusion. "You were getting so good at running. Running from animals in the woods, running across battlefields . . ."

"Running into holes," she laughed. "I've done enough exercise thank you very much!"

"Well, I'm glad to hear you're feeling better. Oh, but I do have a 'Get Well Soon' present for you."

"Ooh, what is it? I like presents!"

Reaching into my jacket pocket, I pulled out a small, round enamel pin. In the center of the circle was a picture of King Robert the Bruce on horseback, a bolt of thunder behind him. Around the circle it said, "1314-The First Adventure."

"What . . . how?" Cassidy stuttered.

"I went online and had it custom-made," I answered, anticipating the question. "I was surprised to see how many people collect them. Anyway, I remembered seeing the pins on your backpack, and you saying how you hadn't traveled anywhere. So, I figured you should have a souvenir of your first adventure. The first of many more to come! Well, in this era that is."

I smiled, waiting for Cassidy to say something. Anything. Instead, she was unusually speechless. I became concerned that I'd said something wrong, but she finally looked up with seriousness and said, "Thank you. This means a lot."

I hadn't meant for the gift to be that big a deal, and I wasn't quite sure why it was. However, my internal questioning was put to rest when she smiled and said, "Well, hand me my backpack so I can put it on!"

As I passed her the bag, Winnie walked through the door. "Hey Ava, I'm glad you're here. David and I have been doing some research on Scotland and we found out some interesting stuff." She handed me a red history book with King Robert the Bruce's name stamped across it. "We were apparently at the Battle of Bannockburn, which was a major turning point in the war with England. Want to know what happened afterwards?"

I hesitated. For the past couple of days, I'd been too nervous to do even a simple internet search. There had to have been many causalities that day. Did I want to know the fate of our friends? *Ava,* I told myself, *if you don't ask, you'll always wonder.* Having made up my mind, I nodded.

"Well," Winnie began, settling into Cassidy's desk chair, "Scotland won."

"Yay!" Cassidy clapped.

"And the guys you met; King Robert, James Douglas, and Robert Keith; all survived the battle and stayed together until the very end."

I felt myself exhale. They'd made it.

"What about King Robert's family?" Cassidy asked. "Did he ever see them again?"

"Yep! His wife, daughter, and sisters were released after the battle in exchange for some English hostages."

"What about the family friend who was captured?" I asked.

Winnie's face fell. "Um . . . they aren't sure, but since her release wasn't recorded, they don't think she survived captivity." Clearly wanting to change the subject, she hurriedly said, "The King of England made it."

"Of course he did," I said scornfully. "I saw him running away from the battle."

"Yeah, we saw him once," Winnie said. "Not a super likeable guy. But that didn't stop King Robert from trying to make peace with him."

My eyes narrowed. "Seriously?"

"Seriously! During the battle, the Great Seal of England and the Royal Shield were taken by the Scottish. King Robert gave it back to King Edward II without even being asked."

"Did it work?" Cassidy asked. "Did they have peace?"

Winnie shook her head. "But there were a lot of other people who changed their minds about King Robert. For instance, Philip Mowbray, who was in charge of Stirling Castle, switched sides and ended up fighting alongside Robert's brother. And I, personally, watched a guy named Alexander switch sides before the battle."

"Alexander?" I asked, recognizing the name. "I saw him! He warned us about the weakness of the English army and urged us to fight."

Winnie brightened up. "Did you hear how we helped him escape?"

"No! You never told me that. What happened?"

For the next several hours; Winnie, Cassidy and I swapped stories, relived old memories, and delved into the lives of those we'd encountered. We were having so much fun together that we didn't even realize how late it was getting until a dorm monitor came by and told us we needed to get to bed.

Quietly, I tiptoed into my room and closed the door, careful not to wake Maci. Setting down my backpack, I changed into my pajamas, grabbed a notebook and pen, and padded over to my bed. Tucked snuggly beneath the covers, I cautiously clicked on a small flashlight. Maci mumbled something, but thankfully stayed unconscious. I exhaled. Opening my notebook, I began to write:

The Lightning Sphere Reports, by Ava Anderson.

CHARACTER GUIDE

Providence Students

Ava Anderson-With a hatred for plaid and a secret to keep, Ava struggles with being the newest student at Providence.

Cassidy McAdam-Full of energy, Cassidy's math and science grades are almost as impressive as her verbal skills.

Winnie Xu-Kind, but often unnoticed, Cassidy's quiet roommate can typically be found hiding behind a book.

Nolan Bradford-A charismatic teen with a "signature smile," Nolan isn't afraid of a challenge.

Victor Salas-With a powerful father and a penchant for mischief, Victor has no problem speaking his mind.

David Levin-Nicknamed "butterfingers," David is most athletic when playing video games and most comfortable when discussing movie trivia.

Maci Vos-Blessed with beauty and wealth, Ava's new roommate feels superior to everyone around her.

Tessa Mueller-Maci's best friend who enjoys her position as the school's gossip.

Kenny Thomas-A student whose hair is great enough to catch Maci's eye.

Providence Staff

Dr. Agatha Hendrickson-The Headmaster who runs Providence with an iron fist.

Dr. Laurence Keller, Ph.D.-Head of the Science Department in the 1970's, his disappearance is that of legend.

Julie Rose-Dr. Hendrickson's bubbly secretary.

1314 Scottish Side

Robert the Bruce, King of Scotland-Seen by many as the rightful ruler of Scotland, King Robert the Bruce is determined to defy the odds and regain Scotland's freedom.

Sir James "Black" Douglas (the "Vampire")-Close friends with Robert the Bruce, James fights for his country as well as to avenge his father's death.

Robert Keith, Marischal of Scotland-One of King Robert's most trusted men, Keith led 500 soldiers on horseback into battle.

Edward Bruce-Robert the Bruce's brother whose deal with Philip Mowbray led to the Battle of Bannockburn.

Agnes-In charge of the kitchen, Agnes is a hearty woman who takes pride in her cooking.

Mr. Crockett-A blacksmith at the Scottish camp.

1314 English Side

Edward II, King of England-The son of a vengeful ruler, Edward II is determined to finish the battle his father started.

Gilbert de Claire, 8th Earl of Gloucester (the "Yellow Knight")-As Edward II's nephew, Gilbert was chosen to command the English vanguard.

Sir Henry de Beaumont, 4th Earl of Buchan (the "French Guy")-Though born in France, Henry has shown his loyalty to England by participating in every major engagement (including the Battle of Falkirk in 1298).

Humphrey de Bohun, 4th Earl of Hereford ("Fake J.G.L.")-Stylish and well-educated, Humphrey may prefer jousting tournaments to battlefields, but is still ready and willing to hold the position of Constable of England and lead the vanguard into battle.

Sir Robert Clifford, 1st Baron Clifford ("Mr. Checkerboard")-One of the most powerful barons in England, Clifford was given the lands that had belonged to James Douglas' father. Though intelligent, he revels in the subjugation of his enemies.

Sir Philip Mowbray, Keeper of Stirling Castle-Having once come close to capturing King Robert the Bruce, Philip's deal with Edward Bruce is his second chance at weakening Scotland's forces.

Alexander Seton-As a Scottish man living on land vulnerable to English attacks, Alexander has a difficult decision to make.

Marmaduke Tweng, 1st Baron Tweng-A veteran warrior, Marmaduke's greatest skill is survival.

About the Author

Erin C.J. Haney is a writer, Christian educator, and history enthusiast living in the friendly Midwest. As a pastor's daughter, Erin developed an early love for the Lord that continues to this day. Her passion for writing became apparent while training at The Second City in improv and comedy sketch writing. Eventually, her many interests culminated in her debut novel, *Rise of the Outlaw Queen.* When she isn't writing or teaching, you will probably find her cutting up vegetables for her two always-hungry guinea pigs, Parker and Josie.

www.ingramcontent.com/pod-product-compliance
Lightning Source LLC
Chambersburg PA
CBHW050844180626
46814CB00007B/2617